In the latest *Tourist Trap* mystery from *New York Times* and *USA Today* bestselling author, Lynn Cahoon, bookshop café owner Jill Gardner contends with a best friend-turned-bridezilla while trying to solve a local historian's untimely date with death . . .

At Coffee, Books, & More, Jill's the boss. But as Amy's maid-of-honor, she can barely keep up with marching orders--and now she's in charge of organizing an epic bachelorette! Adding to Jill's party-planning panic, the South Cove Heritage Society just unceremoniously dumped her historic landmark bid. While vying proposals rush in from a loaded land developer and a pushy travel guide company, Jill finds an unexpected ally in Heritage Society expert, Frank Gleason. But their happy union is cut short when Frank is mowed down in a suspicious hit-and-run. With Amy's big day on the horizon, Jill vows to catch the killer before she has to catch a bouquet.

Also by Lynn Cahoon

The Tourist Trap Mysteries
Murder in Waiting
Memories and Murder
Killer Party
Hospitality and Homicide
Tea Cups and Carnage
Murder on Wheels
Killer Run
Dressed to Kill
If the Shoe Kills
Mission to Murder
Guidebook to Murder
Novellas
A Very Mummy Holiday
Mother's Day Mayhem
Corned Beef and Casualties
Santa Puppy
A Deadly Brew
Rockets' Dead Glare

The Farm-to-Fork Mysteries
Deep Fried Revenge
One Potato, Two Potato, Dead
Killer Green Tomatoes
Who Moved My Goat Cheese?
Novellas
Have a Deadly New Year

The Cat Latimer Mysteries
A Field Guide to Murder
Sconed to Death
Slay in Character

Of Murder and Men
Fatality by Firelight
A Story to Kill

Murder in Waiting

A Tourist Trap Mystery

Lynn Cahoon

LYRICAL UNDERGROUND
Kensington Publishing Corp.
www.kensingtonbooks.com

LYRICAL UNDERGROUND BOOKS are published by

Kensington Publishing Corp.
119 West 40th Street
New York, NY 10018

All Kensington titles, imprints, and distributed lines are available at special quantity discounts for bulk purchases for sales promotion, premiums, fundraising, educational, or institutional use.

Special book excerpts or customized printings can also be created to fit specific needs. For details, write or phone the office of the Kensington Sales Manager: Kensington Publishing Corp., 119 West 40th Street, New York, NY 10018. Attn. Sales Department. Phone: 1-800-221-2647.

Lyrical Underground and Lyrical Underground logo Reg. US Pat. & TM Off.

First Electronic Edition: June 2020
ISBN-13: 978-1-5161-0305-8 (ebook)
ISBN-10: 1-5161-0305-X (ebook)

First Print Edition: June 2020
ISBN-13: 978-1-5161-0308-9
ISBN-10: 1-5161-0308-4

Printed in the United States of America

Homer—Here's your piece of heaven at the beach. May you live forever on these pages.

Acknowledgments

I have to thank all the fans who wrote to me, wondering what happened to Aunt Jackie and, more importantly, asked when the Tourist Trap series would continue. I'd heard stories of how one reader shared his love for the books with his father while they sat in hospice and waited for life to change. It's stories like this that make me realize that although Jill and the South Cove gang live in my head when they aren't off on some adventure, they also live in your head. Thanks for taking the trips to South Cove with me. As always, thanks to the Kensington crew who believed in the Tourist Trap series from the beginning. It's lovely when you work with people you'd want as friends. Thanks also to my agent, Jill Marsal.

Chapter 1

Event planning is a talent that not everyone has in their DNA. No matter what they teach you in high school, it turns out not everyone can do everything. My Home Economics teacher had a section in our senior Family Living class on wedding planning. I would have been better at looking up airline tickets to Vegas. But no, you had to pick out your perfect dress. Set up a caterer. List out your menu. Find a venue for both the wedding—which should be religion-appropriate for you and your future husband—and the reception. She let us go wild. Whatever we wanted, we got.

Then we had to set a budget. And she'd tricked us early on by asking what the future version of ourselves and our imaginary husband did for a living. So the budget was based on the average salaries for those careers. Which she set for you, using some charts she'd found on the internet.

I'd always known that I wanted to be a lawyer. I had one path set for my life. Go to college. Get into a law school. Get my degree. Accept one of many offers for employment. Work and establish myself for five years. Then I'd get married and have two kids. A boy and a girl. In that order. We'd live outside of San Francisco and have a nanny. And maybe an old English Sheepdog. Just to make the family picture perfect. And since I'd chosen a high income lifestyle for me and my imaginary groom, my wedding planning came in underbudget.

In reality, I don't live outside of the city. I live in an old cottage by the sea that I inherited from my friend when she was murdered. Her choices for heirs during her will planning were either me or the money-grubbing nephew. I'm nicer. I'm Jill Gardner, and I was an attorney in the city. But instead of that being my dream job, it turned into a nightmare. And I hit the glass ceiling as soon as I decided my specialty would be family law.

After a weeklong vacation here in South Cove that included a lot of iced tea and conversation with Miss Emily, my friend who later left me my house, I quit my first dream job. And then bought a bookstore-slash-coffee shop here in South Cove. That was almost ten years ago, and I've never regretted changing dreams or careers. But my hatred of event planning has continued. And I was getting pushed to the edge by my best friend's wedding mania.

Today's Business-to-Business meeting speaker was only adding to the whirl in my head. Amy had talked a local wedding planner into coming to talk to the local businesses about setting up South Cove as the perfect destination wedding stop. A topic the bed and breakfast and venue owners were loving. I, on the other hand, was bored out of my gourd.

Of course, not all speakers were going to speak directly to every member of our group of business owners, but it seemed like everyone except me was finding tidbits of gold to take back for their marketing dollars. All I was seeing was carafe after carafe of free coffee getting snatched up by our group.

Deek Kerr was on the clock as our barista for the morning. He sat back behind the counter watching for empty carafes or cookie plates. I'd set out a batch of cookies and gave Amy the invoice to charge the refreshments to the council budget, but when Deek held up an empty plate, I shook my head. If they'd already gone through five dozen, it was time to cut the high. We had to be responsible sugar dealers. He nodded and set the empty plate in the sink to wash later. Then he went back to reading *The Hero's Journey*.

My full-time student, part-time barista was writing his first book. If it was as good as I thought it might be, I might be looking for a new staff member sooner rather than later.

Amy pointed to a note she'd written in pink sparkle ink.

I picked it up and tried to decipher her handwriting. Reading it quietly aloud, I stared at her. "Gunt Toddy?"

Amy shook her head. She leaned close and whispered, "Lunch today, silly."

"Sounds good. If we can ever get out of here." I leaned closer. "I didn't really need to know all about the wondrous world of tulle."

"You need to pay attention. Greg's going to slip that ring on your finger before you know it. Then who's going to plan your event?" Amy looked floored that I was even considering not taking copious notes on the lecture.

"You, Aunt Jackie, this woman I don't know who's talking to us. There are some things I don't need to know." I sighed as Amy pointed to the speaker and pushed some loose pink paper in front of me. I guessed I wasn't getting out of the discussion as quickly as I'd hoped. I gave Deek one last desperate glance in the hope he might need me for something, but when he ignored my unspoken cry for help, I settled down and tried to write down the highlights of the talk.

When we finally met at Diamond Lille's around noon, my stomach was growling and my mood even lower. Probably because I was starving. "What took you so long? The meeting's been over for close to an hour."

I waved away Amy's question and took the glass of tea that our waitress had poured as soon as she'd seen me walk into the diner. What can I say? She knows me. "You're the best, Carrie."

"You're just more predictable than most. Shrimp basket with fries for you and a double cheeseburger, medium fries, and a vanilla milkshake for Amy, right?"

We nodded. I used to be amazed at Carrie's ability to read our minds until I wrote down what I ate each day at the diner and realized I did eat the same thing, time after time. I knew what I liked and I didn't like change. I'd made ordering lunch easy.

Amy still thought it was odd, and she shook her head as Carrie left. "I know you say it's just being a good waitress, but man, sometimes she's creepy good in guessing what I want to eat."

I decided to change the subject rather than get into a discussion of statistics and probabilities. "So why lunch on a Tuesday? Usually you're too busy with city council stuff to get away."

"I wanted to talk to you about the upcoming trip next weekend. You're ready, right? And Greg's still coming? Justin's friends are all bailing on him except for his best man. And he's being cagey about the trip. Who says no to a paid trip to Vegas?" Amy sipped her iced tea, then pulled out a small book covered with a bird binding. It had a latch like a journal or a diary. She opened the book and glanced through a few pages. "Anyway, I was wondering if I should bring the napkin runners to work on while we're there. It wouldn't take more than a day to get them all done."

"Wait, you want us to sit in a hotel room and glue rhinestones on a napkin holder while we're in Vegas? Are you crazy?"

Amy looked up at my face, started to say something, then changed her mind. She focused on writing something in the notebook. "Okay, then, no arts and crafts during the bachelorette party."

Carrie set our food on the table and, after overhearing Amy's statement, laughed. "I had such a good time at my last bachelorette party. We went to a cowboy bar and wore pink cowboy hats, and I rode the mechanical bull. Of course, that was a few years ago, when I married my last husband. If I did that now, I'd break a hip."

"A cowboy bar might be fun." I picked up a fry and pointed it at Amy. "You like animals."

"I do, and that's why I don't attend rodeos. I hate the way they treat them." Amy shook her head. "No cowboy bars. But I'll figure something out. We will have fun."

"Just not too much fun. Remember that you invited Aunt Jackie and Harrold. I'd hate to see them fall off a bull."

Amy picked up her hamburger and took a bite. She glanced at the notebook, and all of a sudden, I knew what she'd had planned.

"You were going to have us finish the decorations for your wedding. At your party." I shook my head. "The parties I've been to have been all about getting the bride drunk, not getting things done. Have you ever been to one?"

"Of course I have. I just thought that this might be more fun. We could order in room service and watch movies on television. And it wouldn't be all weekend. I'm sure we could get everything done in ten to fifteen hours, max."

I took a deep breath. I was going to regret this, but it had to be done. "I'm the maid of honor; I'll plan the party. Just be ready to have fun."

"But what are you going to do?" Amy demanded.

I shrugged, dipping a shrimp into the cocktail sauce. "It's going to be a surprise."

And it was going to be a surprise, even to me.

And that is how I ended up in charge of a wedding-related event after I'd messed up my own fake wedding in high school.

Walking home, I kicked myself for opening my mouth. Arts and crafts wouldn't have been that bad of an activity. As long as I didn't have to use a glue gun. Those things hate me. When I got home, I pulled the mail out of the box and flipped through it as I paused at the front door. I guess it was just the right time of the year, but my mail was filled with wedding flyers along with the multiple credit card offers. I flipped through the mail, separating it into two piles: throw away and take a peek at. The peek ones were bills. I put those on the kitchen table and threw the others in the recycling.

I opened my laptop and Googled Vegas bachelorette parties. Some of the choices made me blush. Others made my pocketbook run and hide. Seriously, why had Amy thought having the party in Vegas was a good idea? She was a beach girl. She liked sand and surfing and bonfires. All things I could have set up just down the road with no problem at all.

I sighed as I pulled out a notebook and started making a list. I'd write down the ones I liked, the ones I loved, and the ones that weren't bad. Then I'd rank them in terms of practicality and costs.

When I'd said I'd plan the party, did that mean I'd pay for it as well? I'd have to Google that too. Maybe it was a requirement of being a maid of honor. The dress had already set me back more than a few dollars. Now I needed to pay for fun and games for everyone?

Maybe my aunt would know. I glanced at the clock and picked up the phone.

"Coffee, Books, and More, may I help you?" My aunt had on her customer voice. Friendly, easy to talk to, and approachable.

"Hey, it's me."

A barely audible sigh came over the line. "What do you want, Jill? The store can get by without you checking in every hour you know, right?"

"I'm not checking in. I called to see what you knew about bachelorette parties. Does the maid of honor have to pay for it?"

"I take it Amy talked you into handling the event?" My aunt spoke to a customer about a children's book. I waited until she finished.

"No. I mean, yeah, I'm handling it, but it was my idea." I had a bad feeling about this.

My aunt laughed. A mix between a tinkle and a snort. "She told me she was going to get you to handle it this morning. I didn't think you actually had a choice in the matter. Amy can be pretty persuasive."

"Pretty tricky, if you ask me." I sighed. I hadn't even seen the trap my friend had laid. "So do you know if I have to pay for it?"

"No, you don't. Ask Amy what your budget is. That way you're both on the same page and you don't get stuck with stuff she didn't want you to order. But you should offer to chip in some money. Just because you're friends." My aunt spoke to another customer. "Look, I've got to go. I'll leave you a package under the counter. Open it tomorrow as soon as you get here."

"What is it? Did you get me a kitten?"

Now the laugh was more relaxed, lighter. "Not even. Besides, Emma would have a fit. She'd be jealous. I've got to go. I've got a line of people waiting for me."

I kind of doubted that, but I hung up the phone. Tomorrow, I'd worry about the party, and I'd stop by City Hall at lunch to see what Amy had in mind and what her budget was. It only seemed fair.

I glanced at my golden retriever, who was sitting by the door, watching me. She probably wanted—no, needed—to go for a run. And I was too good of a pet owner to squash her dreams.

Greg would be home soon, and we'd be grilling pork chops and corn for dinner. We tried to eat together during the week most days because if he was going to get called out, it would probably be on a weekend. We'd been living together now over a year and it was good. We were good. I knew it was time to consider the next step. But he hadn't asked and I hadn't hinted.

I liked our life exactly the way it was. For now. I hoped Greg did too. I ran upstairs to change for the run. The pile of bills could wait.

When we got to the beach, I questioned Amy's Vegas choice again. And cursed myself for offering to plan the party. What was I thinking? The beach was empty, so I unsnapped Emma's leash and shoved it in my pocket. Then we started running.

The best thing about running on the beach was getting out of my head. I worried a lot. I worried about the store. About my aunt. About Greg, when he was on a case. About us as a couple when he wasn't. You could describe me as a serial worrier. Or maybe slap a label on me, like OCD. It wasn't like I checked the light switch three times before I went out of a room, but I did think about what part of my routine I'd missed when I'd left the house.

Today, Amy's party was my focus. I didn't have a plan. And I loved a plan. I made plans for everything, including the shop's future goals and any upcoming trips Greg and I were taking, even just for the weekend. So first step, who had she invited? I knew my aunt, and Mary, and probably Darla. But what about Esmeralda? What about Tina, her boss's wife? I'd call Amy as soon as I got home. I'd pull out a notebook and get this party started. Well, the planning part of it anyway.

I was so lost in my planning that I hadn't noticed the stranger walking toward me. Emma's bark drew me out of my thinking mood, and I paused next to her, watching the man move toward us.

He was dressed in plaid shorts and a crew neck T-shirt. His salt-and-pepper hair was cut short, yet long enough to blow around a bit with the breeze. He waved and smiled at me and, with the action, just above his chiseled, cut jaw, two dimples appeared. Well, wasn't he just a cutie pie? When he was within earshot, I nodded. "Sorry about having her off the leash. I thought we were alone out here."

He put his arms out to soak in the beauty of the day. "I bet you get a lot of days out here without any tourists ruining your run. She didn't bother me at all."

Emma sniffed the man's hand, then her tail started wagging. In dog terms, that meant the man wasn't a serial killer. Or at least he hadn't killed anyone lately that Emma could discern. My dog tended to like most people, so I didn't totally trust her judgment on new arrivals. "Glad to know. You staying in town?"

"Yes, I have a room for at least a week at the South Cove Bed and Breakfast. Lovely place, although the room is a bit fluffy for my tastes. Unfortunately, I don't have a Mrs. to enjoy the décor." The smile came out again.

I wondered if I was being hit on. It happened so rarely since I was living with the South Cove police detective. No one wanted to challenge Greg. I decided to move this conversation along and finish my run. "Well, have a nice stay in South Cove. I run the bookstore coffeehouse downtown, so if you're in need of some reading material, I can hook you up."

"I brought a bunch with me, but if I run out, I'll stop by. Actually, I'm here to write a story. About you, Jill Gardner. Well, actually, about your house."

His words made me freeze. He must have seen the concern in my eyes when I heard him call me by name.

He reached into his pocket and pulled out a business card. I'd been expecting a gun or, maybe, a knife. I took it, not liking the way my hand was shaking. I looked down at the information and almost laughed. "You're an author?"

"I write those travel books everyone buys. The local-charm books? I'm working on a series of historical places not on any register, and your house and the Mission Wall came up during one of my interviews." He held out a hand. "Mike Masters. That's my real name. I write under several different pens and, of course, I ghostwrite for a lot of other name authors when I have time in my schedule. But I love writing these history books. I think so much is being destroyed without us ever knowing what our past could tell us."

I put the card in my pocket and watched him. The man seemed honest enough. "You said someone told you about the Mission Wall. Was it Frank Gleason?"

"No. That guy is as tight with information as Fort Knox. He thinks everything he works on is confidential. But it was someone in his office. I can't tell you their name because I don't want to get her in trouble."

"But it's a woman?" I took stock of the man in front of me. He probably did really well at signings. He was good-looking and personable.

He rubbed the side of his face with his hand and grimaced. "I'm really not good at keeping secrets. I'd make a terrible spy. But don't make me tell you. I'd feel horrible if she got fired or something because of the stupid rules."

I wanted to say that sometimes rules weren't stupid, and that I didn't want people coming by the house to find the rumored hidden treasure.

Mostly because what treasure there had been, I'd already found. "Look, I appreciate your honesty, but let me be up front too. I don't want to talk to you. I don't want the Mission Wall to be in a travel guide. And I don't want you in my life anymore. Thanks for asking, but the answer is no."

As I started to walk away, he called after me. "Keep the card and think about it. You might change your mind."

I didn't think that was possible, but I needed to warn Greg that Mike the writer was in town and wanted to interview us for this book. Even though Greg didn't actually own my house, he'd be shown as the owner or friend of the owner. No, it was better for us to have a united front from the first day of this.

United front. I kind of liked the idea. Emma and I finished our run and headed back to the house to get some things done before dinner. Normal, everyday, couple-type things. I'd like our lives to be boring for a few weeks, or even months. A girl could hope, right?

Chapter 2

Greg grabbed the pile of mail I'd left on the kitchen table and did his own sort. I paid the bills for the house, then he sent me his share every payday. We also had a couples travel account that we put extra money in when it came. Right now, we were saving for an Alaskan cruise. My aunt had made noises about wanting to go with us, but I was hoping to keep it just a couple thing. As soon as she asked Greg, though, I knew it would be a done deal. The man may fight criminals for his day job, but he was no match for my aunt when she wanted something.

"Did you see this letter from the Heritage Society?" He held up the business-sized envelope.

I stopped chopping veggies for a salad and reached out for the envelope. "Let me have it."

Greg handed it over and I put it up to my head. "I see the following. 'Dear Ms. Gardner. The commission is significantly behind in our historic site evaluation and processing backlog. Please be sure that we are doing everything possible to complete your evaluation as soon as possible due to funding limitations. We will be in touch again in six months to let you know the status of your application. Feel free to contact us directly with any questions. Yours in magic, Mathilda Parker.'"

"Almost a nice Potter reference, but I don't believe her last name was Parker. That was Spider-Man." Greg snatched the letter from the spot on the table where I'd tossed it after my show.

"I don't know why I even let anyone talk me into this. The decision takes so long." I went back to chopping the cabbage for the salad.

"Because you're a good citizen, and if there is proof that the wall in your backyard is part of South Cove's history, you'd move heaven and earth to save it." He opened the letter himself. "I hate to say it, but your psychic powers are way off the map."

"What do you mean?" I didn't even turn around. It was probably a letter stating the commission was moving or something.

"The society has issued a decision on the application."

I turned, my chef knife still in my hand. "And?"

"I'm sorry, Jill, they said they don't have the funding to approve the site." He kept reading. "Weird, though; they don't say if it was a historic site or not, just that they don't have the money to chase it this year."

"They spent four years on hold just to tell me the funding is low?" I put the chopped cabbage in a bowl. "What a waste of tax dollars."

"It says you can reapply next year if you want." Greg set the letter down and came behind me and wrapped his arms around me. "Are you okay?"

"I'm fine. It was stupid anyway." I felt tears on my cheeks. "I don't mind, except for Miss Emily. If this land is actually a historic site, it should be protected."

"We could just do it ourselves." He kissed the back of my neck. "Maybe get some press on the issue?"

I groaned, thinking of the writer I'd just blown off at the beach. "Speaking of media, there's a writer who's going to try to get an interview with me or you about the wall. I was thinking our answer should be no comment. But now that the Heritage Society has bailed, maybe we should think about talking to him. What do you think?"

"I think I'm not getting my barbeque party patio." He glanced out the window to the backyard. "It's too bad too. The spot would have been perfect for private evening dinners and a little canoodling."

I started to laugh. "Did you really just say canoodling?"

He gently bit my neck, then let me go. "What can I say, I've been hanging out with Harrold too much these last few months. Are they still coming for dinner Sunday night?"

I finished the salad and cleaned up the sink. "As far as I know. Aunt Jackie's been busy with inventory. And her shift has really picked up since the chain bookstore in Bakerstown shut down. I hate seeing any bookstore close, but we are gaining a lot of business. Especially the online orders. Deek's new platform has paid for itself the first quarter out. I may have to give that kid a raise."

Greg's phone buzzed. He picked it up and looked at the text. "Sorry, I've got to go. You go ahead and eat. I'll grill something when I get home."

"Something wrong?" Toby Killian, Greg's part-time deputy and my part-time barista as well as the guy who rented out the shed-turned-apartment in the backyard didn't usually bother Greg at night unless it was important. Like a murder serious. And we'd had more than our share of those in the last few years for such a little town.

Greg smiled. "Kind of. At least it's serious to the sea lion."

"Excuse me?" I put wrap over the salad and put it in the fridge. I wasn't that hungry, and if I waited a few hours, we might still be able to have dinner together.

"You'll see it on the news. Toby says there's already a television crew out there. Look, I've got to go save a wandering sea creature. And you say my job's boring." He kissed me as he grabbed his keys and left the house.

"At least it's not a dead body," I told Emma as she watched him leave through the back door.

She barked a response that could have meant she agreed with me, but probably meant "where's my favorite guy going?"

I grabbed a bottle of water and went over to the table to work on Amy's party again. I would figure this out before Greg got back, send an email to Amy for approval, and make the reservations. I'd planned two weddings, my fake one and the one for my failed marriage. I could plan one little party for a few women.

I opened my notebook and made a list of the things I knew and the things I didn't. The list of didn't knows was way longer. I sent an email to Amy with my questions, then started sorting through options.

I still hadn't heard from Amy and my head was pounding by the time Greg came home. He came in through the kitchen door and stopped short when he saw me. "I thought you would have been in bed by now."

I closed the laptop and put the notebook on top of it. "Nope. Project Bachelorette Party is kicking my butt. Do you know how many options there are for a female-themed party in Vegas? If we were all twentysomethings, I would have been done by now. But I know my aunt's coming, so our ages range from twentysomething to Aunt Jackie. That's hard to plan for."

He got out the pork chops and frowned when he saw two still on the plate. "And you didn't eat."

"I forgot. And now I have a headache to prove it." I stood and grabbed the salad and French bread, slicing off a bit. I spread peanut butter on it and started eating. I was starving. "So tell me about the sea lion."

He glanced at his watch. "Let me put these on the grill and you turn on the television. Channel Seven will have the story. I'll fill you in while the meat cooks."

I opened the fridge and grabbed two bottles of beer. "You want one?"

"I do." He grabbed the chops and the tongs and headed out the door. "I'll be right back in."

We had a small television mounted on the kitchen wall now. Greg's idea. When I was home alone, most of the televisions stayed off unless I was watching a movie or a cooking show, or if I just wanted some noise in the house. Greg, on the other hand, always seemed to have some sports game or the results of a game on. He also watched the news a lot more than I did. I really didn't want to hear about all the negative events around us. He wanted—okay, maybe needed—to be informed for his job. I liked to think that my piece of the earth was happy and easy-going. Kind of like a free Disneyland without the rides. Well, maybe like Disneyland if no one was murdered and I didn't get involved in solving cases all the time. Okay, maybe not like Disneyland at all.

He came in a few minutes later and I turned down the volume. The murder mystery cop show was just finishing up and the main character was running through a dark alley, getting ready to save the day. He glanced at the screen, then grabbed his beer and sat next to me.

"Some kids called the station about five. Reporting a sea lion over in Patterson's soybean field." He took a swig out of his beer, leaning back in his chair. He'd taken his gun belt off and stored the gun in the safe we kept in the mudroom. It was such an automatic thing now, I didn't even notice he did it anymore.

"Wait, isn't that the field on the other side of the highway from the beach? How in the world did he get over the road?" I was trying to imagine the spot Greg was talking about. The beach at that place was the sunning place for the sea lions when they came in for the day. There was a gate keeping people off that section, allowing the large creatures not to be bothered by tourists and humans wanting a picture. Greg had to rescue people who'd ignored the signs and the fence at least a few times a month.

"Yeah. From what I could tell, he came up the service road and through the gate, which was wide open. Someone had cut the chain and dropped the lock. I'm going to have to get that replaced in the morning. Right now, we have it wired shut. Then the guy just inched his way about the length of two football fields over the road and into the field."

"I can't believe some car didn't hit him."

The local newscasters came on the screen and Greg turned up the volume. "Here's the piece."

I watched as the large sea lion moved back toward the ocean and through the field. Toby was on one side of the guy, Tim on the other. Greg was talking to the reporter, a few feet away. "We appreciate the call from this guy over here." Greg pointed to the kids. "It's great when young people step up to keep our wildlife safe."

He grunted next to me, and I eyed him. "You think the kids are the ones who broke open the gate?"

"I think this kid had a lot of friends and they were the ones who started this chain of events. That kid was the only one who stayed around and called it in when the sea lion got out of the fence. He had the good sense to call for help, even if it meant he was in trouble."

I watched as the camera panned over to the teenager who stood watching, his face pale and his eyes downcast. "What's going to happen to him?"

"He'll probably get a commendation from the mayor for good citizenship. Which is going to make him feel even guiltier. But maybe we caught him early from a life of bad pranks gone wrong." He stood. "Pause that a second. I need to flip the chops."

When he came back, we finished watching the video clip. I turned off the television. "You looked like a hero on television."

"Yeah, Marvin is going to hate that. Even with the election over and his seat secured for four more years, he's convinced he's going to lose the spot to me as soon as I actually run for mayor." He sipped his beer and nodded to the fridge. He stood and kissed me. "You get the rest ready and I'll go get the chops. I'm starving. And I'm really glad I don't have to eat alone tonight."

That brought a smile to my lips. My hero boyfriend. It sounded like a title to one of the romances Sadie purchased by the truckload.

* * * *

I realized the next morning that we really hadn't talked about Mike the writer and if we wanted our house to be on the unofficial register of historic stops on the central California coast. Greg had left early to take care of the paperwork on rescuing the sea lion. Which was surprisingly extensive. He'd told me that there were at least five agencies where he had to file his official report, not including the South Cove Police Department. And he had additional deadlines to meet, so it would be a morning filled with paperwork. We were still on our winter schedule at the shop, so I didn't open until seven. So I had time to run with Emma before walking into town for my shift.

Have I mentioned how much I love living in South Cove lately? When I worked in the city, I had an apartment, but I still had to take a bus to the stop closest to the law firm's building, then walk from there. Which was great on nice days. I started to hate the rain after a week of downpours, when I'd had to carry dress shoes in my backpack and schedule my arrival at least an hour before my first meeting so my suits would have time to dry out a bit. My hair just pulled into a tighter curl, so there wasn't anything I could do with it. Humidity plus curly hair equaled frizz. My boss called me Rosanne Roseannadana on those days, and I'd had to Google the reference, but she hadn't been wrong.

My first customer was sitting at one of the café tables outside when I arrived. He handed me his credit card. "Large coffee and a couple of those brownies to go, please. And I need the next book in this series. My plan is to have this one done at lunch."

I took the card and glanced at the Lee Child book. "I'll look it up and make sure I get you the right one."

"Tell Deek thanks for the recommendation. I'm loving this series. I can't believe I hadn't tried him earlier." Jay—the man's name was Jay, I remembered now that I saw his credit card—was an attorney in the city. We'd talked about my time at the firm, but where he was involved in tax and business law, his income kept him happy working the long hours, including a crazy commute. Yet he still made sure he made time for himself, including his pleasure reading.

I hadn't taken great care of myself until I'd moved here. Owning a bookstore had given me a lot of free time to think about what I wanted out of life. Well, it had until my aunt had moved to town and taken over managing my store and my life.

I started the coffee machines, tracked down the next-in-series book for Jay, and had his coffee and brownie breakfast packed up with a receipt in less than five minutes. I took it back outside, where he was still reading. I set down the bags and cup and handed him back his credit card, along with his receipt and a bookmark. He sighed.

"Thanks Jill. I guess it's time for me to start adulting for the day." He slipped the bookmark into the hardback and then pulled out his wallet. "You're not hiring for this shift, are you?"

"I doubt I could afford your salary needs." I straightened the chairs at the other tables and took the rag I'd brought out on the tray and washed the tabletops. "And this shift is taken. I'm not giving it up for anyone."

"Actually, it's for a friend's daughter. She's looking for a job to supplement her grants while she finishes her degree. I'm not sure what exactly she needs, but can I send her your way?" He stood, waiting for my answer.

"I'm not sure if we're hiring right now. But have her send us a résumé and mention your name. I'll talk to my aunt to see if we're going to need some summer help or not." I paused at the door. "We don't hire a lot here. She'd probably have better luck finding a job in Bakerstown."

"I'll mention that too. Her dad has a place just down the highway. She's back home after a bad breakup. My friend has asked me for the name of a good criminal lawyer, just in case he goes ballistic on this guy."

I knew he was kidding, but I understood the feeling. Sometimes murder was just about how big a jerk the victim was when he was alive. Not to say I condoned any type of murder, but I did understand it. "I know some of those too. The criminal lawyers, I mean, not the homicidal fathers."

He chuckled. "I got it."

When he left, I did my opening chores, thanks to a laminated list my aunt had made for every shift. Just in case we forgot what to do from one day to another. I went back to the message whiteboard, where we all left messages for one another. The board was clean except for the words, *Work Your Open and Close List.* Thank you, Captain Obvious. I picked up my pen. *Are we hiring for shifts yet? Jay's friend's daughter is looking for a job.* Then I signed my name, just in case my aunt didn't recognize my handwriting. Okay, so maybe I was related to Captain Obvious.

Then I grabbed an urban fantasy magic book and a fresh cup of coffee and sat down to read, waiting for the next customer.

When Deek showed up at eleven, I'd only been disturbed twice. Once for a commuter who needed coffee because her husband had forgotten to buy coffee at the grocery store run last weekend. And a family who was here on vacation and looking for reading material. The daughter, who must have been eight, came to the counter with no less than eight books. The son, a year or so younger, had two. The parents mirrored the kid's buying habits. The wife bought four paperbacks and a new release hardback from a woman's fiction author I loved. He brought up a well-reviewed book on the life of Lincoln. My aunt would be pleased at the number of books sold this morning. My shift was usually more of a coffee-buying one.

Things were good in my world. I mean, there was the whole Amy party planning thing and the fact that nobody official cared that I had the last original wall to the South Cove Mission in my backyard, but all in all, things were great.

I decided I'd finish up the party planning this afternoon. And tonight, while we had dinner, Greg and I would make the decision about what to do or not do about the wall.

Chapter 3

The sense of peace and tranquility didn't last long. My aunt came down five minutes into my reading time and thrust a paper at me. "Did you see this?"

Carefully placing a bookmark to save my spot, I set down the book regretfully and took the papers. "I don't know if I saw this or not. What is it?"

"The Council is raising our fees for the business group. They are blaming us for the price increase because our charges for the room and refreshments are so high." My aunt put on her reading glasses and pointed to a paragraph in the middle. "I've gotten five emails today asking why we're fleecing the city."

"I only charge out what they eat. Maybe if people didn't have two brownies, the monthly costs wouldn't be so much." I stared at the paperwork. Reading the letter, it was clear the message was that the fault was ours, not the council's. Way to make it not about the City Council's decision and shift the blame. "I'm calling Bill. He needs to fix this. If we get the entire community mad at us, our sales will plummet."

"Whatever you need to do, do it quickly. I don't even want to open my email program." Jackie glance around the empty shop. "You go make your calls. I'll watch the shop. I'm so worked up right now, I might as well be doing something productive."

I grabbed the book and my coffee. I guessed I'd have to finish reading at home after my run. I dialed South Cove Bed and Breakfast as I walked. A recorded voice told me that although my call was very important, the staff was all working on making current customers' stays amazing. The recording invited me to leave a message. Instead, I hung up and grabbed my tote. I paused at the counter where my aunt stood and checked the morning receipts. "Deek will be in at noon. If I take care of this sooner, I'll be back and finish my shift. Just don't worry."

"I really didn't need all this hostility today. Harrold's trying to teach me to meditate, but every time I start, I get pulled into drama. Why is my life so complicated?" Aunt Jackie held up a hand. "Don't answer that. I don't want to know what I'm doing to keep the chaos going. Plausible deniability is a valid excuse, at least in my eyes."

I was proud of myself when I didn't even giggle as I left the office. I'd negotiate a new regular charge for the monthly costs and the Council would send out a new letter. I'd never seen them be so heavy-handed in their negotiation tactics before, but maybe Bill had just been in a bad mood when he wrote the letter.

Mary was in the kitchen when I knocked on the back door. She opened it wide and pulled me into a hug. "I'm so glad you came. It's been crazy here and I haven't even had a chance to call Jackie to tell her the news. How did you find out?"

"The Council sent a newsletter." I extracted myself from Mary's bear hug.

Mary's face filled with confusion, but then the buzzer went off on the stove. "Hold on a minute, that's my banana bread. I'm confused, though. The Council sent a letter about Bill's father?"

Something else was going on and we were having totally different conversations. "No, about the Business-to-Business group's dues. What happened to Bill's father" I watched as she pulled out two loaves of bread that smelled like bakery heaven.

"Grab some coffee and sit down. I think we both need to start this conversation over." She turned off the oven and returned to the table, where her own coffee sat with a large reservation book. "Now, tell me what's going on."

I went through the discussion with Aunt Jackie that morning and the comments she'd been getting from the business community. "I've never seen her this upset. I don't understand why Bill would point fingers like that."

"He wouldn't. This had to be Alice Carroll's doing. That woman hates Jackie and, by extension, your coffee shop. As part of the City Council, she's always trying to get the meeting moved to Lille's diner, but Lille refuses to take on the management of the group, so it never gets to the point where the group even votes." Mary walked over and cut two slices of the still-warm bread, bringing them over on plates with a cube of butter.

"I don't understand. Why wouldn't Bill stop this?" I pointed to the letter. "Or at least warn us."

"Bill's been out of town trying to get his father set up in a nursing home. We'd bring him here, but the doctor says he's too weak to travel. I knew we should have done something last summer, but you always hope it's not the time, you know." Mary bit into her bread, holding up one finger while she chewed. "I've been running the business since last Monday. He didn't make the last Council meeting, so that must have been when Alice struck. He should be coming home this weekend, but until then, you'll just have to deal with the comments. Besides, I've never seen either you or Jackie back down from a fight. What's the difference in this one?"

"She's tired, I think. This whole thing with the fake Uncle Ted has her questioning herself." I sipped my coffee. "Do you think Bill will be able to fix it?"

Mary smiled, and I knew she was thinking of her husband. "Bill will fix this. He's got a little touch of Superman gene. That's why I miss him so much while he's gone."

I reached out and patted her hand. Her wedding set sparkled in the morning sunshine, even though it had to be thirty years old. Mary and Bill were my aunt's age, and I considered them more than just friends. "If you need anything, call and I'll come over or send Greg. He'll be happy to help."

"He's a good man. Strong, thoughtful, and crazy in love with you. When are the two of you going to make this playing house permanent?" Mary's gaze searched my face for any tells, but actually, we hadn't talked about marriage, not for a while. Greg had been married before, as had I, and we were both a little skittish.

"Someday. There's no hurry." I finished my coffee. The conversation was getting deep. Time to bail.

"I thought that about Bill's father too. Life sneaks up on you. And it changes in a heartbeat." She held up her hands in surrender at the look. "I'll get off the subject, just think about it."

I thought about Mary's advice as I walked back to the shop. I needed to calm Aunt Jackie down and draft a standard response we could shoot back when we got challenged. I'd handle that. My aunt was just as likely to tell the person what to do with their opinion than cut and paste a reasoned response that told everyone this wasn't our fault and we'd be working with the Council to revert the dues to the prior level.

At least that was the plan.

I was almost at the shop when Frank Gleason from the Heritage Society rushed up to me. His hair was sticking up all over his head and his buttoned-down shirt wasn't tucked in or even buttoned correctly. I barely recognized him from the focused, put-together man who'd come to interview me about the South Cove Mission Wall.

"Miss Gardner, please tell me you haven't received a letter from the Society yet?" He licked his dry lips as he watched me.

"You mean the one where you explained how you didn't save a vital part of South Cove's history? Yeah, I got it." I was glad I got to complain in person. Lack of funding was a common complaint in the California government system, but typically, nonprofits didn't use the excuse. Of course, it could still just be pending. I guess I should be glad that the wait was over, even if the outcome wasn't what we'd hoped.

"Just ignore the letter. The project won't be taken off the pending list. I had a lack of judgment and hit the wrong button." He took out a handkerchief and wiped his face. "You'll get a correction letter in a few days."

"Really? I don't have to reapply or anything?" Now I felt a little guilty for raising my voice. If he was actually helping, I'd get more flies with sugar.

"Yes, yes. I'll handle everything." He glanced over his shoulder and checked both ways down the street. He turned back to me, narrowing his eyes. "Just don't do anything stupid."

Entering the shop, I saw my aunt watching me as I walked in. "Okay, so I've found out what's going on. Bill's going to fix it when he gets back."

Aunt Jackie pointed to the retreating figure who was now walking down the side of the road toward his Smart car. "Is that Frank? What did he want? Don't tell me the preservation of the wall finally got approved?"

"Not yet, but it's not been blackballed from the process. Which is where we were this morning." I handed my aunt the loaf of banana bread that Mary had sent with me. "Mary sent this over for you."

"I'm not eating carbs." She pushed the packet back at me.

"What are you talking about? Why aren't you eating carbs?" Out of the corner of my eye, I could see Frank talking on the phone, paused outside his vehicle. He really should take that call inside. South Cove didn't have much traffic, but our streets were pretty narrow.

"I'm losing weight for the wedding. I want to be the same size I was when I married your uncle." She glared at the offending banana bread. "Maybe we should just give it to Deek or Toby. Men don't seem to have the same problem with carbs."

Just then, I saw a large black Ram come screaming down the road. He was going way faster than the posted speed of twenty-five MPH. I saw Frank turn, his face draining of color, then the black truck blocked my view. The sound of the thump when the truck hit the older man hadn't been blocked, though. I dropped the bread and swung open the door. "Call 911 and get an ambulance out here."

Not waiting for a reply, I took off running. As I did, the black truck backed up and sped down the road.

"The plate is A5490B. A5490B." I kept repeating the license plate number over and over, hoping I'd remember it. My phone was in my jeans pocket and I pulled it out, hitting speed dial for Greg. Like I'd expected, I'd gotten his voice mail. "Black Dodge Ram truck. Double tires in the back. License plate A5490B."

I hung up and tucked the phone back in my pocket. I was at the scene now and my breath was coming fast and hard. I tried to slow down my breath as I looked at Frank. His eyes didn't see me, and as I reached out for a pulse, I knew I wouldn't find one.

The ambulance came seconds later. Of course, it felt like hours that I stood there, guarding the body and trying to keep traffic from the side of the road where Frank lay. Greg followed the EMT guys, and he put his hands on her arms.

"Are you all right? You're not hurt, are you?" He turned me left, then right, then ran his hands through my hair. "Did you hit your head or fall?"

"I wasn't involved in the accident. Aunt Jackie and I were at the window of the coffee shop. He came up and talked to me. Said he was going to fix the issue with the wall. Now he's dead, so there won't be any fixes."

"Which means you needed him alive. I'm so glad. I was worried I was going to have to arrest you for murder."

I narrowed my eyes, watching his face. When he didn't smile like he usually does on a bad joke, I rubbed my face. This couldn't be happening, not in a little town like South Cove. "You don't think it was just an accident?"

"You don't either." The words were calm and definitely not a question. He led me over to the sidewalk where a bench had been placed. "Sit and let me deal with this. I'll take your statement a little later."

I did what he told me. Soon after the EMTs arrived, the van with Bakerstown Memorial Home on the side arrived. Doc Ames climbed out. The doc was owner/manager of the local funeral home, as well as the county coroner. Because there weren't a lot of suspicious deaths in our little corner of the world, it worked out well for his life. Especially because it was just him and a part-time secretary, who also helped with hostess duties at the larger funerals.

He pulled on a canvas fishing hat over his graying hair and moved slowly to the side of the road to check the body.

My phone buzzed and I answered, turning away from the sight. "Hi, Aunt Jackie."

"Should I come out and sit with you? Why don't you come back to the shop and sit out of the sun?" I could see my aunt standing at the bookstore window, watching me.

"No, stay there. I'm coming inside. I'll let Greg know where I am, but Doc Ames is here and I just don't want to watch anymore." And I didn't want my aunt to see this.

A clicking sounded on the other end of the line. "Is he dead?"

"Yeah." I caught Greg's gaze and pointed to the bookstore. He nodded. Which was one of the great things about living with someone. They knew what you were saying, even if it was just a hand gesture or head nod. "I'm on my way inside. I can't believe that truck just kept going."

I didn't get a response, and when I looked up, my aunt was no longer in the window. And my phone was dead. I wondered if she'd heard anything I'd said after telling her I was coming inside.

Deek had already arrived and was set up at one of the tables. He came in a lot to write during off hours now that he was working on his first novel. He wouldn't tell me what it was about. He'd gone through a few first chapters and then dumped it all. He stood and hurried across the room to meet me. His blond dreadlocks had a pink tinge to them. "Are you okay? That must have been horrible."

"I'm fine. I just can't believe he's gone. He was just talking to me, then he got hit by a truck? What is going on?"

"Probably a drunk driver. Someone who was still partying from last night." My aunt went over to the counter and poured a cup of coffee. "Here, drink this. It's been a crazy morning."

"That's for sure." I eyed one of the brownies sitting in the case.

"Fine, have a brownie too." She glanced at the clock. "Your shift is almost over and Deek's already here. Why don't you go to Lille's and grab some lunch instead of feeding a sugar high?"

"Greg wants to talk to me. So I'll stay here until he comes in. He's probably going to be too busy to eat too." I rubbed my temples, trying to will away the headache I knew was coming.

"Well, keep yourself busy instead of just sitting there, freaking out." My aunt nodded to the back room. "We have new books that just came in this morning. You could put them into inventory and then stock the shelves."

"I was going to do that on my shift." Deek closed his computer. When he saw the look my aunt gave him, he stopped short, laptop under his arm. "Of course, I could do something else."

"I'll put them into inventory and you can stock the shelves. I think we had a pretty big order this week. You might have to change up some of the shelves to make room." I ate my brownie in two bites. Then I stood with my coffee and went around the counter. "Let me know when Greg comes in."

Aunt Jackie put her hand on my arm as I passed her. "You couldn't have changed anything. You weren't close enough to stop that guy."

"I know. And what could I do against that large a truck anyway?" I gave her a quick hug. "But thanks for checking on me."

Back in the office, I grabbed some scissors and started opening boxes. We had a large trash can we put the box stuffing in when we unpacked. Most of the stuff got reused; we sent out a good number of mail orders. Or we did since we'd hired Deek. The guy had a knack with online marketing. If we ever taught him the accounting system or signed over the bank account for his use, he'd be the one employee Coffee, Books, and More couldn't do without. So we kept him out of the long-term planning as well as the accounting. We had to have some secrets, right? I'd unpacked all the boxes and was about halfway through keying the books into our inventory when Greg walked into the office.

"Glad to see you keeping busy, but shouldn't you have left hours ago? I called your cell to see if you were at Lille's or home. When I didn't get an answer, I came here."

I pushed back my hair out of my face and blew off a line of stuffing that hadn't wanted to leave when I'd picked up the book. "You said to stay nearby."

"I didn't mean—" Greg pulled off his baseball hat and put it over his head backward. "Anyway, sorry if I wasn't clear. Come have lunch with me. I can take your statement and eat. And I'm starving."

"You really should eat more than doughnuts for breakfast. You need solid food." I grabbed my purse and walked out toward the coffee shop area. "You need to take better care of yourself."

"I have a girlfriend to gripe at me for these things. Why would I change?" He picked up my tote and groaned at the weight. "How many books are you taking home? Thank God we have built-in bookshelves."

I smiled at his mention of our home. Our bookshelves. Our lives. "Let's go, then, before your other girlfriend finds out about me."

Chapter 4

We were halfway through lunch when I realized Greg hadn't asked me anything about the truck or what I'd seen.

"We really need to see a show while we're there. There are a lot of stars that retire to the Strip and just do shows for the bigger casinos. I can't blame them. It must be hell living out of a suitcase most of the year to tour the new album." He finished off his mashed potatoes. I'd noticed that he typically ate those first, then his meat, and, finally, his veggies. Greg belonged to the Clean Plate Club, but the way he got there was totally different from my eating process.

I set down my fork and watched him.

Finally, he met my gaze. He waved his fork at my chicken burger and fries. "Aren't you hungry?"

"Why aren't we talking about what happened to Frank? I thought that's why we were doing lunch today."

He stopped eating, picked up his water, and took a long drink. Then he took my hand. "The reason we're not talking about what happened is, I wanted just a little time with my girl before I go headlong into this investigation. You know how things can get when I've got an important case going. I don't come home for dinner. If I come home, I'm late, and I leave early. I just wanted one hour where I could pretend that the next few days aren't going to be total crap."

Now I felt like a jerk. I squeezed his hand. "Sorry. I should have trusted you. I just want to clear my head of the memory, and right now, I'm trying too hard to keep everything in my head. I don't want to forget something important."

"You already gave me plate and vehicle information. If we're lucky, the BOLO I put out before I left the station will have him in some jail north of us by the time lunch is over." He nodded to my plate. "So are you going to eat that and talk to me about sweet little nothings?"

"Sure, why not." I cut my sandwich in half so I could get my hands around it. No matter what happened in my life, I could always count on Lille's food being outstanding. And this chicken sandwich was no exception. "Did I tell you I'm planning the women's section of the party?"

He choked on a sip of water. "Are you kidding? Does she even know you?"

"Of course she knows me. We've been friends forever. Oh, you were dissing my mad party planning skills."

"Honey, you hate planning the book events that come to your bookstore. You already told me you put all the event planning onto Deek as soon as you hired him."

I shrugged, enjoying my sandwich. "He's good at it. It's a shame not to use an employee's talent when you can."

"That's your story…" He laughed, pushing away the empty plate and leaning back in his chair. He checked his phone.

"You're going to have to get going, right?" I knew that look. Playtime was over.

He drew out his notebook and clicked his pen. "Tell me what happened."

* * * *

After Greg left, I stayed at Lille's to finish my lunch and, just because I was feeling a little depressed, I ordered some apple pie à la mode. I'd run tomorrow. By the time I got home the mail had come, and I took the pile to the back porch, where I could hang out with Emma after she made the yard safe from any roving wildlife or bunnies. My dog hated bunnies. I think they teased her when I was at work and she could see them from the back window.

I flipped through the mail and opened a large envelope with Keller Construction on the return address. I unfolded the papers and started reading. Emma had joined me, so I read aloud just so she could know what was going on. "'Dear Ms. Gardner. We are starting the process for developing a large water park in your area. Due to your house's proximity to the highway, it's in a prime spot for us to consider purchasing and building our project on your land. If you are interested in selling, please contact me and we can set a time to talk about our offer.'"

I folded the paper back into the envelope and tossed it onto the swing. "What is it with all the drama around the house lately? First that writer stops us and wants to write about the wall. Then the wall isn't going to be approved, then maybe, then Frank dies, and now someone wants to buy the house? Way too much stuff going on around here for my taste."

Emma barked, but it was at Toby coming in the driveway. He hustled over to his shed apartment and unlocked the door. I watched him disappear into what could only be described as an ultratiny house. Twenty minutes later, he came back out, still dressed in uniform and headed back to his truck.

I was waiting for him at the gate. "What's going on?"

"Jeez Jill, you scared me to death." He tried going around me.

"Hold up, buddy, what's going on, why are you here?" I studied his uniform; it looked way too clean.

He visibly relaxed. "Oh, that's what you want? I thought, I mean, I got stains on my shirt. And since I'm pulling a doubleheader, Greg let me come home to change before I start patrolling."

"Good idea." I held my hand up to his chest, and he looked nervously down at it. "I only need one more thing."

I let the statement hang in the air. Toby looked at me suspiciously. "What?"

"Tell me how the investigation is going. Did you find the truck?" I knew I must have looked like a news junkie looking for the next hit.

He stepped around me. "No way, no how. Greg gets testy when I tell you about investigations, and I'm coming up on my annual evaluation. I don't need things like 'failure to protect classified information' showing up and lowering my chance of getting a raise this year. I like my job."

When he saw the glare, he added, "I like both jobs. You're putting me in a bad situation here."

He was right. I shouldn't have asked. I reached down and petted Emma. "Sorry, it's just I was there when it happened. It feels closer somehow because of that."

Toby paused, leaning over his doorframe, watching me. "I know. And from what I heard, you couldn't have done anything. He was probably dead as soon as the truck hit."

"Poor Frank. It's crazy that some random event takes someone out like that. It's like that *Final Destination* movie—when it's your time, it's your time." I watched to see how Toby would react to my words. And I wasn't disappointed.

"Well, yeah, there's that." He didn't meet my eyes; in fact, he turned his head away and climbed into his truck. He started the engine, then leaned out the window. "Look, you can't tell Greg I told you this, but we don't think it was random. He had threats on his computer at his office and at home. Nasty ones. And that's all I'm saying."

"I don't know if that's better than just being unlucky or not." I waved to Toby as he backed out of the driveway. My phone rang and I glanced at the display. "Hi, Amy. What's up?"

"Just following up on the table decorations. I know you said next week, but you've had the stuff for more than a month. I have the afternoon off. Maybe I should come over and help."

I groaned. I was in a quandary. If Amy came over, she'd see I hadn't made any progress on the decorations since the last time she'd come by and set up my kitchen as craft wedding central. But if I said no, I'd have to actually get them done next week. And I wasn't sure that even I could get these done in a month's time by myself. I decided to take the bullet. Besides, maybe she'd feel sorry for me because I'd witnessed what had happened to Frank.

"Sure, come on over. I'd appreciate the help. I haven't gotten as far as I'd hoped." Which wasn't a real lie. "Besides, I've got questions before I can finish the party planning. When should I expect you?"

I could hear papers being rustled on the other side. "I'm leaving now. Marvin and Tina took off for a long weekend, so I'll just put the phones on forward."

Wednesday was kind of early to be leaving for the weekend, but the fact that Marvin was out of town worked in Greg's favor. He'd have to keep the prosecutor in the loop, but not the mayor. Which meant that maybe he'd even come home for dinner, or at least to sleep. Sometimes I thought Greg took his law enforcement duties just a little too seriously. But I had to admit, he was good at it.

"See you in a few." I disconnected and went into my office, where I'd stashed the box holding the materials and the almost-empty plastic tub that Amy had given me for the completed items. There weren't any more completed than when I put the boxes away a couple of months ago. I'm really good at procrastinating when I don't want to do something. Besides, the wedding was still three months away. I glanced at my wall calendar and turned the page. Okay, make that two months away.

I just hoped we finished this today. I really needed to get at least one thing checked off my list. Too many items were building up. Especially things I wasn't good at. And housework. Housecleaning—like mopping and cleaning surfaces—went on the list once a month and got checked off. Then the next month it went back on. Sometimes Greg and I took a weekend and went through the whole house. The good news is, we weren't slobs, so it stayed pretty okay during the times in between. Unless Emma got into something. Then all bets were off. I took the boxes into the kitchen and got out treats I'd brought home from the shop. Then I made coffee. Greg wouldn't be home for dinner. Maybe Amy would stay over and we could make a frozen pizza or something.

Amy came in the back door, wedding binder in hand. At least it wasn't as huge as my aunt's. I was beginning to get a complex about all the wedding plans being made all around me. But then I'd think about how perfect our lives were right now and I'd push the thought away. Marriage meant babies. And more housecleaning, because babies would put anything in their mouths. And Emma; what would she do with a baby around? And what would it feel like to even be pregnant? I pushed all the worry questions away and went to greet my friend. She could deal with all those things first. Then I'd have a role model to ask questions.

Maybe it was a coward's way out of the fear, but I'd grab any lifeline in the storm.

"Hey, Amy." I gave her a quick hug. "Thanks for coming by. I have to say, I don't think I get how to make the decorations quite like you did."

She set down her stuff and glanced into the box. "It's my fault really. I know how you are around crafts. You just don't get it."

"I get it," I shot back, but then I looked into the almost-empty box again. A box Amy had counted on me to fill months ago. "Okay, so I'm not crafty, sue me. I've got some ideas for your party, though." I poured myself a cup of coffee and grabbed the notebook I'd started making notes in. "Like I said, I have a list of questions."

She pushed the planner book at me. "There's a section on the party in there. Who I invited, who said yes, etc. I did some brainstorming with Justin a few weeks ago about what we might like to see. But don't worry about him. Toby's handling his party. Tim's staying back to watch South Cove while Toby and Greg are gone for the weekend."

I took the book and started writing down her notes into my notebook. "Thanks, this really helps."

Amy plugged in two glue guns, then sat down with her own coffee. "I almost forgot. Are you okay? Esmeralda said Jackie was the one who called in the hit-and-run. But you were first on the scene, right?"

"Yeah. Not my best memory." I kept my head down and continued to write. "You know who it was, right? Frank Gleason? The history guy who was working on getting the wall certified as historic?"

"No, Esmeralda didn't know. She thought it was a tourist, not a local." Amy started putting together the doodad for the table. Driftwood, shells, a piece of moss, and a sprinkling of sand made up the centerpiece. It was pretty, in a natural, classic way. Justin had wanted to add mini surfboards with their names on it with a heart. We still had them, just in case Amy changed her mind. "I guess this really wasn't a good time to do this."

"Actually, it's a great time. Greg's off investigating the accident. So you being here and keeping me busy helps. I feel so bad for him. He was on his phone, talking to someone. Well, yelling at someone, when this truck just swung over and hit him." I compared the two lists and then went through my questions to make sure there wasn't something else. "I'm going to work on this a while, if that's okay. Then I'll help you finish up."

"That will work. I hate the fact he was angry when he passed. I bet whoever he was talking to feels really bad about the last words they had." Amy adjusted the moss before adding the glue. "Passing over should be soft and easy. A natural path to the other side, as Esmeralda calls it. Not angry and violent."

I thought about Amy's words as I went through the list of ideas I'd brainstormed for the party. Then I started researching available venues and costs. Amy turned on the stereo, and we worked for a couple of hours in the quiet. But something about what she'd said bothered me. Who had he been talking to and why were they fighting? Did it have anything to do with the lack of movement on the wall certification? I'd told Greg that Frank was going to change the status of the wall back to pending. But what had made him change it in the first place? Or had it been someone else? So many questions, not enough answers. I bookmarked the three choices I had for the party. I'd call the places tomorrow to make sure they could do what Amy wanted and then closed my laptop, moving it over to the kitchen desk. Then I turned the notebook to the back and started writing down everything I knew about Frank Gleason and his death.

When I'd finished, I closed the notebook. Amy was watching me. "What?"

"You're investigating what happened to Frank, aren't you?"

I shrugged, standing up and putting the notebook on the desk with the computer. "Maybe I just wanted to write down some issues that don't make sense. It's not a real investigation."

"Keep telling yourself that." She pushed a piece of driftwood toward me. "Ten to go and we'll be done. When we are, I'll buy dinner at Lille's."

The thought of fried chicken and mashed potatoes was a much better idea than frozen pizza, but I'd really have to run tomorrow. Eating out twice in one day wasn't great for my diet. "Sound good. But it's weird that the first-ever hit-and-run murder we have in South Cove is Frank, right?"

"Weird stuff happens. That's why I'm so excited to be starting my life with Justin. You never know when things are going to blow up on you." She looked pointedly at me. "You need to live your best life now."

"What are you trying to say? I *am* living my best life. I love the store. I have Aunt Jackie with Harrold. I have great, if nosy, friends. And I have Greg and Emma. What else do I need?" I picked up the piece of deadwood. Mine wasn't pretty, like the one Amy was working on. In fact, it looked like it had been burned and thrown away. Maybe if I covered up that section with some moss, it might look a little presentable.

Amy took the moss and placed it away from the blemishes. I frowned at her but went ahead and glued it there. It was her wedding.

"You need to settle down. You and Greg need to make this official. Maybe even start a family?" She handed me the sand to shake over the wood. "We could raise our babies together."

Something about that just made me shudder. It wasn't that I didn't want kids; I did. But not now. Somehow, I knew that the marriage conversations were just going to get stickier as our friends became "official" couples. I didn't meet her eyes when I answered, focusing instead on the little glue lines I was making on the driftwood to add the glitter. "I don't know if I'm ready for kids yet."

Chapter 5

Dinner conversation at Diamond Lille's with Amy ranged from why I was crazy to not want kids now, when I was young enough to keep up the energy level, to an in-depth discussion on who was sitting next to who at the reception. It felt like this conversation was on a repeat loop for Amy. The big problem was who she was going to make sit by Marvin and Tina. She had to invite the mayor, mostly because she worked for him, but no one we knew would be looking forward to sitting for a meal, not to mention a reception, with Marvin.

I longingly remembered the times we'd met in the past and not talked about the wedding. I know it wasn't charitable or kind, but I was just about fed up.

As we left, I paused at Diamond Lille's Celebrity Wall of Fame. The newest addition to the wall grinned out at me from his photo, not like the man I'd met on the beach. "He cleans up pretty nice."

Amy glanced around the room. "Who? I don't see anyone we know."

I pointed to the picture. "That's the author I met on the beach. Didn't I tell you? He wants to write about the Mission Wall in one of those tour guide books. I'm kind of worried that it will bring people to hang around my backyard. Emma would go crazy."

"What does Greg say?" Amy held the door open and we walked out into the soft evening air.

"Well, after we got the letter saying the project had been kicked out of the funding pool and we could reapply, I think he was all for getting some press on the area. Then Frank told me to ignore the letter, but now he's gone, so I'm not sure what I'm going to do." I narrowed my eyes as I watched my friend adjust her tote for the walk back home. "Why did you ask about Greg's feelings?"

"If you guys are a long-term couple, eventually, that's his home too. In fact, it's his home now anyway because he's living there. He should have a say." She grinned at me as we headed down the sidewalk toward her apartment over the bike rental shop. "Of course, if you got married, it would be his house too."

"No, it's mine. It came into the relationship before the marriage so it's separate property." I rolled my shoulders, because I was getting pretty tight talking about all this marriage stuff. "You forget, I used to do California family law."

"But you'd want to share, wouldn't you?"

Amy's question haunted me as I walked home. Would I want to share? Would I put Greg's name on a house I inherited free and clear and cash flowed to any repairs or remodeling? I'd been married before; actually, both of us had. I didn't want the finances to get in the way of the relationship. And, with the Miss Emily Fund—my personal name for the large inheritance my friend had left me when she passed—I didn't need Greg's financial assistance.

When I looked at Amy and Justin, and even Aunt Jackie and Harrold's upcoming wedding plans, I saw the planning for the event, not the mingling of financial lives. Did this mean I was no longer my aunt's beneficiary? Had we added her to the ownership documents last year like we'd talked about? I'd wanted to protect her at the time, but now, I was wondering if doing that had threatened my own situation. If Aunt Jackie passed first, would Harrold be my new partner? I needed to talk to both Greg and Aunt Jackie to see what the expectations were. I didn't care about the money per se, but I needed to know where I stood, and protect my future self's nest egg.

Staring out on the ocean as I walked home, I wondered if I was just being my usual literal self. Did I need to trust that the people in my life had my best intentions at heart? Or should I actually talk to them about my fears? This would be a most uncomfortable discussion, so I wanted to choose the former and just trust.

Trust, but verify. It had been my boss's favorite saying at the law office.

I resigned myself to having the conversations. It would be foolish not to, and I would be kicking myself if I didn't do it and something went wrong. I put away the fears and worries until tomorrow. But before I relaxed, I put two notes in my planner: *Talk to Greg. Talk to Jackie.*

Then I called Emma, and we went out to the back porch with a book and a bottle of beer. The wedding decorations were off my to-do list, thanks to Amy, and it was time to celebrate.

* * * *

The next morning, Greg had come and gone without me even noticing. Which meant the investigation was keeping him busy. I made a note to take him coffee and muffins when Deek came in for his shift. It was Toby's day to work, but with the murder, I knew he'd probably have called Deek in to cover because he would have gotten additional hours from Greg. I knew where I stood in Toby's eyes. Coffee, Books, and More was definitely his second job.

I took Emma for a run, then filled my travel mug and headed into town. There weren't a lot of people up and about at a few minutes before six. Most of the businesses, besides Diamond Lille's, wouldn't open until ten. But as I passed by a small gallery owned by a group of artists, there was one woman out on the small café table sketching in her pad. I'd met her at one of the Business-to-Business meetings. Tia something. She drank coffee from a Diamond Lille's travel mug and frowned as I walked up. "Good morning. Lovely day to sketch."

"It would be if I wasn't arguing with all the coop members. They're not very happy about the increase in the Council dues. We may not join up next year. And we're not the only ones thinking about quitting." Tia shook her head at me, like I was the problem.

"Look, it's not our fault the dues are going up. When Bill Sullivan gets back in town, he's going to fix this. I'm only charging what the catering costs me. I don't get any bump from having you all in my shop except for my salary for running the meetings. And I'm getting exactly what the woman who ran it before me got." I knew it was stupid to argue. The artist had her mind made up on who was the bad guy. And in this case, it was the hand that fed her. Literally. "I'm sure this will get corrected soon. I'm not the enemy."

"I want to believe you. But until we get something else from the Council, it appears that you were the reason our dues went up. I'm not the only one who's saying it."

"I guess I could walk door-to-door and explain my side of things, but honestly? I've got a business to run. I can't stop rumors. All I can do is go to the source and tell them they're wrong. Which I did. Think what you want." I left her watching my back as I made the way up past City Hall and then crossed over the street to my shop. Seriously, people needed to get a life. I couldn't believe there was nothing going on in town that the rumor mill couldn't play with besides the increase in the Council fees and our fictional part in the raise.

Irritated with the whole thing, I sat at my desk and typed an email to Bill. I hated bothering him while he was with his dad, but I was tired of being looked at as a money grubber. Maybe he could send out a retraction now and follow up when he got back.

My email showed a quick response. Too quick. I opened the email from Bill, which kindly explained he was out of the area and unable to accept emails. He'd respond when he returned, in a few days. So much for my quick fix. According to Mary, he'd already been gone a few days, I wondered what his anticipated return date really was and if I could hold off blowing a fuse at people until then.

I poured another cup of coffee and added a lemon bar to my plate, along with the brownie I'd already chosen for breakfast. Then my first customer arrived and I was too busy to worry for over two hours.

By the time the last customer left, I was in a better mood. I opened my notebook and started a list of all the things on my mind. Last week, this would have only been those decorations Amy and I finished up last night. Well, and when Nick was coming home from school so I could put him on the schedule and cut some of my hours. But he wouldn't finish up classes for a couple of weeks, so I shot him a quick email, telling him to do great at finals and to reach out when he knew what day he wanted to start his summer shift.

Then I put a follow-up for two weeks on my calendar and drew a nice black line through his name on the to-do list. I wrote down Amy's decorations and did the same. I wrote "reach out to Bill" and did a thicker line through that, and put a reminder in my online calendar for late next week. Glancing at the clock, I saw it wasn't even nine and I'd already crossed three things off my worry list for the day. I deserved a treat. I dug into the lemon bar and sighed at the sweet/sour goodness. Then I continued my list.

The wall was a major confusion. Frank had told me not to worry or reapply, that he'd handle it. But that wasn't going to happen now. I put a note on my calendar to talk to Greg as soon as I had a chance and refile the paperwork. I paused after I wrote that. Had Amy been right? Was it a good sign for my growth as a person that I was taking his input into my future plans? Or was I giving up control?

I ate half the brownie while I mused on these questions, then decided to just let it be for a while.

Next on the list was Amy's party. I sent out emails for party quotes and availability. I wrote down my top three choices, then kept a spot open for costs and availability.

I had just gotten back to Frank's murder, which really shouldn't have been on my worry list in the first place, when Deek came in.

"Hey, Boss Lady." He poured some coffee, then sat down next to me at the counter. "You okay? Your aura's all mixed up, with a rainbow of colors."

"Well, that's exactly how I feel." I smiled at my barista, who claimed not to be a psychic like his mother, but he read people better than anyone I knew. Including our town's fortune-teller and my neighbor, Esmeralda. "How is your day going? The words coming well?"

Deek groaned and flipped his blond dreadlocks out of his face. Today they had a spattering of multicolored beads weaved into them. "The story doesn't want to follow the outline. Every time I sit down to write, the muse takes me somewhere else. Don't get me wrong; it's a great idea, but it's not what I had on the outline. I keep having to rewrite my outline to fit the new plot points."

"Do you?"

He looked at me strangely, sipping his coffee. "Maybe you didn't understand. What I'm writing isn't on the outline. The characters, they're taking on this whole life of their own. If this keeps up, the book won't be anything near what I planned it to be."

"And the problem is?" I finished the last of the brownie, knowing I was going to have a killer sugar headache if I didn't get some real food in my stomach to counteract eating dessert first.

"Sorry, I forget you're not a writer. Maybe I can go back to the beginning. I write out the outline of what the book is going to be about. Then I write the story." He spoke slowly, like I was in elementary school and hearing about sentence structure for the first time.

"No, I get what you're saying. I've sat in on enough author talks that I know you're following the plotter method of outlining your story down to the last detail. Then you write the book. But have you considered you're a pantser? Maybe your subconscious knows what the book is going to be, but you have to write the chapters before you do?" I sipped my coffee, watching his reaction.

"I thought I had to write an outline? My creative writing professor told us we had to start there or the story wouldn't ever get done. The way I'm going, the story's not going to be done for years." He got up and got himself a brownie. Which made me smile. If my employees weren't emotional eaters before they joined the staff, I tended to train them to become one by modeling the behavior.

"Look, this process might work for your professor, but I bet if you went online to any writer's group and asked who plotted and who pantsed, you might find a lot of people who write like you do and still produce books." I glanced at the clock and stood to fill a couple of travel carafes of coffee, then packed up a box of treats, making sure I charged them under "Jill's account." It could have been marketing, but my aunt took a dim view of me charging the marketing budget for treats I took to my boyfriend's workplace.

Sometimes she ruined all the fun.

"Think about it. Maybe your outline is a working document and you don't have to rewrite it every time you add to the story. Or, if this is for a grade, write the outline when you're done with the book. I promise you no one, except maybe your publisher, will ask for your synopsis once you're out of school." I grabbed my tote and loaded up the goodies. "I'm out of here. Going to City Hall for a quick chat with Greg."

"Hey, Jill?" The emotion in Deek's voice made me turn around to face him. I took a step forward, but paused. "What's wrong?"

"You're kind of wonderful, you know that?" Deek's back was turned to me, so I had to strain to hear the words. "I can't believe you knew exactly what to say."

"I've been serving coffee and suggesting books for a long time. Getting into the heads of the authors we invite into the store is kind of a hobby. You would have gotten there. I just pointed the way." I turned and pushed open the door, then held it open for a group of Toby's girls from the cosmetology school. I knew they wouldn't be disappointed with Deek, but I was glad I hadn't had to take over Toby's shift. They didn't like finding out they drove fifteen minutes for just coffee. Now, coffee and flirting time was fine. My lips curved into a smile as I headed across the street to City Hall to get my own daily dose of flirt on.

Esmeralda shook her head when I walked in. "He just left for Bakerstown. Some interview for this new case."

I held up the treats. "Okay if I put this in the break room, then? I hate to have Sadie's treats go to waste."

"You're kidding, right? Those will be gone in less than thirty minutes." Esmeralda took off the wireless headset that made her look a little like Cher in concert. "Of course, whatever I eat will go to waste, but *my* waist, not the trash can."

"You look amazing." I followed her into the break room, where she cleared a table that had been covered with newspapers, magazines, and one lone, empty soda bottle. "How have you been?"

She stacked the newspapers and magazines on another table, then tossed the bottle toward the recycling bin. "These guys are slobs. And for some reason, they think they can get away with it here. I'm going to have to have a talk with Tim again about throwing his bottles away."

"How did you know it was Tim's? Did it have his aura?" I wasn't sure how this worked, but I was impressed.

"Tim's the only one who drinks lemon lime soda. The others are either Pepsi or Coke people. Tim's been saving his money, so it's a no-name brand as well." She laughed as I put down the coffee and treat box. "No woo-woo here, just observations and putting together the clues. You do the same thing."

I shrugged and opened the box, offering it to Esmeralda. "Maybe. But like Greg always tells me, I'm not an investigator."

Esmeralda took a cookie, then nodded to the box. "You have time for a short break with me? I haven't talked to you in weeks. And I heard you were the one who found Frank."

I sank into the chair and glanced out at the empty reception station. "You sure you have time?"

She pointed to the earphones. "Not only will they forward calls to me, it also chimes when the door opens. We're fine back here. But stop stalling. Are you good?"

I took a cookie. I needed real food, but it was an oatmeal cookie, so that should have some nutrition. I'd stop at Lille's on the way home and get a huge salad to go. "I guess. I mean, it was a shock to see him there. I'd just talked to him, and then he was gone. I don't think I've ever experienced that before."

"That abrupt a leaving may cause his spirit to hang around. I could try to reach out to him for you if you want. No charge, just a favor for my neighbor," she said, focusing on the cookie instead of watching my face. Although she probably was still watching me. "I can schedule a session at my house tonight. Are you ready to accept your gifts and reach out to the other side?"

Chapter 6

Being part of another séance scared the crap out of me. Esmeralda had spearheaded one on Halloween, when we'd all gotten together to visit a haunted house before it was torn down for a development of high-end condos. Even though it was supposed to be all fun and games, things had happened that had led us to finding a killer we didn't even know was around. Talk about a cold case. The thought of trying it again, without all my friends around and to reach a guy who'd I'd just talked to in real life, made me shiver.

"That's really nice of you, but maybe we can leave that for now. I'm not sure what I'd ask him if we did try to reach him." It wasn't that I believed in Esmeralda's gift, but after the Halloween incident, I had to believe there was some type of power there. Besides, I didn't like hurting anyone's feelings, especially someone I considered a friend.

"You are still having difficulties understanding my gift." She held up a hand when I tried to argue. "Again, not woo-woo, but I see it on your face. You still think I'm a whack job."

I shook my head. "Actually, I am trying to respect your talents. Deek has some of the same traits, but I think he's just very talented in reading people. Me especially."

"Deek is very special. Did you know he was my godson?"

We talked for a while about my newest employee, but when the phone rang, I made my escape without telling Esmeralda what was really bothering me. I wanted to talk to Greg and Aunt Jackie first. Get my role tied down in both of those relationships. I could only hope that my directness wouldn't be seen as aggressive. Sometimes I could be like Emma with a bone. Especially if something was bothering me.

Instead of going outside, I went down the hallway to where the mayor's office and the community meeting rooms were situated. I could ask Amy if she wanted to go to lunch, but I'd probably be turned down. She had a rule that she limited her eating out to one or two days a week. Which I thought was just silly. Sometimes, I ate at Lille's every day, especially if Greg was out of town or I was out of ice cream at the house.

She was at one of the long tables near the front window and talking to a tall, good-looking man I didn't know. I hesitated. I didn't want to interrupt, but I really didn't want to go back to the police station and go out that way. Esmeralda would probably be off the phone and would corner me about what I was upset about. At this point, all I wanted was a way out of the building. One where I didn't have to talk to people.

Amy must have sensed my presence as she looked up and smiled. "Hey, Jill, what a coincidence. Aaron and I were just going over land areas open for development. He mentioned the area around your house. I told him you weren't interested in selling." She studied me. "That's correct, right? You wouldn't sell Miss Emily's house to be torn down, would you?"

"Not my plan." I stepped forward to greet the developer. I might as well take care of this issue; the guy wasn't just going to let me get away with ignoring his letter. "Hi, I'm Jill. I should have called when I got your letter, but things have been crazy here. Like Amy said, I'm not interested in selling the house."

"Aaron Presley. Yeah, Mom had a wicked sense of humor and a devotion to fifties music. I think she married Dad based on his last name alone." His blue eyes twinkled and when he smiled, he had a dimple that made his square jaw even more attractive. "I'm afraid I was led to believe you might be interested in looking at an offer.

"Not sure who would have said that." I shrugged. "I love my house. I can see the ocean from the front porch. It's relaxing."

He chuckled. "I get that. Your little town has been just outside the crazy California build zone for years. I'm afraid that's not going to be the case soon. I know several other developments that are looking at your area. In fact, your mayor has been attending a lot of development conferences that are calling your area the next Malibu."

I wanted to tell him that Mayor Baylor rarely spoke for the town. Most of the time, he was selling his own interests. I was pretty sure he'd been buying up property in the area and holding it just for the big development offer. Me, I like the small tourist town feel South Cove had developed over the years. Adding in high-rise condos and blocking off beach access would change the entire feel of the area.

"Yeah, sometimes he has a different vision of South Cove." I tried not to add the criticism of our city leader to the comment. Time to get off this subject before I put my foot in my mouth. "What are you interested in building? Maybe Amy could suggest some different areas?"

"He's bringing in a water park. One with all the crazy slides." Amy's false cheerfulness told me everything I needed to know about what she thought of the idea. Being a surfer, she liked her beaches remote and accessible to all. "I've mentioned the fact that Bakerstown has a large amount of land near the coast just north of here."

He shook his head. "Too far for the city visitor. We already built a park just north of San Francisco. The weekend visitor rates are through the roof. People want a safe place to have a little fun. And there are just too many issues with wildlife near the shoreline for the ocean to be a viable, kid-friendly area."

I saw Amy's mouth open and I kicked her leg, just a bit. She was going to go off on this guy. She believed in having kids out in the real world. And if they understood how to share an area with wildlife, like the sea lions who liked to sun themselves just down from our community beach, that was even better. This guy wanted to isolate kids with plastic slides and chlorinated water for their safety.

I didn't like water parks. It felt too artificial. Especially with the Pacific just minutes away from where we stood. But my aunt had always taught me to be nice to strangers. Especially those who didn't pose a threat. "Well, I hope you find a suitable area. I'm sorry I had to be the one to give you the bad news about my house."

He studied me, probably wondering if I was just holding out for a really good offer. "Well, at least I know now. Are you sure I can't just give you a ballpark figure of what we'd be prepared to offer? I'm sure we'd be able come to an agreement that would be beneficial for both of us."

I shook my head. Even if the wall didn't get approved, I loved my house. Okay, so maybe *especially* if the wall area didn't get approved. I hated the idea that I might lose a part of my remote sanctuary to history buffs. Of course, there might not be that many visitors who wanted to see a three-foot-high remnant of a mission that was long gone. "Seriously, I have no plans to sell. If I did, I'd just have to buy or build another house, which would be a hassle."

He considered me. "You may reconsider. Here's my card. I'm in town for the next week or so while I finalize a spot. I'll be at the Castle, so don't hesitate to call, even if you just want to grab a drink or dinner and talk about the piles of money I have to spend on just the right spot."

I laughed and reached for the card. "I can't see me changing my mind in the next couple of weeks, but if I do, I'll call."

His eyes turned smoldering, and he held on to the card just a second longer than necessary. "You could just call because you wanted the drink or dinner. No strings attached."

Greg's voice came from behind me, and I felt his arm going around my waist. "She already has someone to eat with, but we appreciate your offer."

Aaron's gaze left my face and focused upward on Greg's face. "Sorry, man. No ring, so I didn't know."

"No harm. She would have turned you down anyway." Greg held out a hand. "Greg King, lead detective for South Cove Police."

"Aaron Presley. I'm a developer looking for land for a new water park here in town. Jill's house is in the perfect spot and meets all our requirements." He shook Greg's hand, all friendly and salesmanlike.

"Except it's not for sale." Greg amended Aaron's statement.

Aaron let his gaze drop to mine, then he nodded. "That's what I've been told."

The silence held for a long minute, then Greg stepped around me and took my hand. "I'm ready for lunch if you are."

I nodded and looked at Amy. "We'll catch up later. Nice to meet you, Mr. Presley."

"Aaron, please. And it was very nice to meet you both." He nodded at me and Greg as we walked out of the building.

"That was weird," I said after the door closed and we were on the sidewalk heading to Lille's. "Thanks for extracting me. You don't have to take me to lunch if you don't want to."

"Esmeralda said you needed to talk to me. That something was wrong." He glanced behind us at City Hall. "Then I find Mr. Slime hitting on you. I guess she has a good sense about things."

"Mr. Presley," I corrected him, "wants me to sell my house. He had no interest in me besides that."

"I'm not sure that's true." Greg shrugged. "But I'll let my caveman attitude drop if you say so."

"He would have taken me out, I'm sure of that, but the house would have been behind it." I ran the conversation through my mind. "He said someone had told him I'd be interested in selling. Do you think it was Mayor Baylor?"

"Probably. The guy wants to turn this town into North LA, just so he can make money on the real estate holdings he has. He has no clue how special South Cove is."

"That's the truth." As we walked into Diamond Lille's, Carrie handed us menus and pointed us to our favorite booth. I tried to put the conversation behind me, but something was nagging at me. "Don't you think it's weird that I've had three contacts about the house, two on the wall and one to sell, in less than three days?"

"I didn't say South Cove wasn't a desirable real estate market. Everyone wants to enjoy the laid-back lifestyle." Greg studied the menu, then closed it. "But I don't want to talk about the house anymore. What's going on in your world that Esmeralda thinks you're so upset about?"

I set the menu down and sighed. "Amy got me worrying about the future last night. And I realized that if something happens between us, things needed to be said."

"I know, you love me. And nothing's going to happen to either me or you. You really need to get over not being able to say the words, though." He smiled up at Carrie, who had delivered two iced teas. "Carrie, you read my mind. Thanks."

"No problem. I suspect you're having the stuffed meat loaf plate? Even though it's beautiful outside. I only crave meatloaf when it's raining." Carrie arched an eyebrow.

"You do know me. And, because I'm probably not eating a 'good' dinner, I need something with some staying power. Besides, Tiny makes the best meat loaf I've ever had." Greg glanced at me. "What about you, cupcake?"

I snorted at the nickname. "I'm having baked tilapia with a side salad and Thousand Island on the side. I think I ate my weight in sugar this morning."

"So no milkshakes?" Carrie asked.

We both shook our heads, and she took the menus. "I'll have that right out. You're early for the lunch rush, so you should be able to get back to making South Cove safe soon."

After she left, I shook my head. "I'd be offended if my afternoon plans didn't surround me on the swing, finishing a book."

"No party planning? Or solving Frank's murder on the investigation?" He put a hand over his heart. "Who is this woman and what did you do with Jill?"

"Funny. I'm waiting for quotes and availability on the party venues. And I didn't realize you'd classified the hit-and-run as a murder." I sipped my tea, watching him.

"You and I both know it was. I just can't figure out why." He leaned back as Carrie set a plate in front of him and then a salad in front of me. "That was quick."

She shrugged. "Apparently, Tiny has the two of you figured out as well. Jill, the rest of your meal will be out soon. Do you need anything right now?"

"We're good, thanks." Greg waited for Carrie to leave. "One thing, though: Did Frank ever talk about an ex-wife?"

"Frank was married? Wow, I didn't see that coming. The guy seemed so rigid and devoted to the work." I took a bite of my salad. Not fried fish or french fries, but good. And exactly what I needed.

"Yeah. Apparently, he was married five times. And dating someone currently. His landlord told me about the new blonde that started staying the night about a month ago. Of course, he didn't mention a name to his landlord. But he did blush beet red when the guy brought her up when Frank dropped off his rent check." Greg took a large bite of the meat loaf and nodded. "Tiny's on his game today."

"Why did the landlord bring her up to him?" I reached over with my fork and took a small bite of the meat loaf. It was good. I should have ordered that.

"My guess is he told him he'd have to raise the rent. That Frank's cost was based on single occupancy." Greg moved his plate closer to him and out of my reach. "Tonight, I'll be reaching out to the ex-Mrs. Gleasons and trying to find who was auditioning for the role of number six."

"You're saying I shouldn't wait up." I smiled at Carrie as she took away my empty salad plate and exchanged it with the fish. Tiny had added cauliflower mashed potatoes to the plate, as well as a side of green beans. I guess he didn't want me going away hungry.

"Probably not." He studied me. "Are you sure you're not getting into the investigation? Are you holding back on me?"

"Yes, I did start a paper list, but I haven't talked to anyone besides you and Toby, and no one has told me anything. Except what you just did. I still can't believe he was married once, not to mention five times. I guess you never know about someone's private life. Is the working theory that one of the wives drove over him due to late alimony? Do judges even assign alimony anymore?"

"Not usually, unless there's a large discrepancy in individual funds." He finished his real mashed potatoes before I could do a taste test with my fake ones.

Individual funds: that's what I wanted to talk to Greg about. I set down my fork, wiping my mouth with my napkin. "Greg, there's something I want to get straight."

He frowned and set down his own fork. "Is this going to ruin my appetite?"

"I don't know." I shrugged and looked at the half-eaten lunch. "Should we wait until we're done eating? I don't want you to be late for an interview or something."

"Now I've got to know. Tell me you're not kicking me out because I work too much. You knew who I was when we got together." His phone went off and he groaned. "Sorry, I have to take this."

I nibbled on my food while he talked to who I thought was Doc Ames on the other end of the phone. Luckily, they didn't talk much about the specific details of the autopsy or I wouldn't have been eating either.

"Sure, I'll drive in. See you in thirty." He hung up the phone and wolfed down the meat loaf.

"Look, it's not about..."

He held up a finger, stopping me. "I can't take the time to talk. Just put a pin in this and I'll wake you up before I go into the station tomorrow and we can talk. If you don't want me out tonight."

"I don't want you out tonight." I felt frustrated. "Look, you need to know what I'm asking, so you won't..."

"Think the worst? Honey, that ship's already left the harbor." He stood and kissed me on the head. "I won't think the worst until we can talk. That way I can still pretend everything's all right and I can focus on this investigation."

He threw two twenties on the table. "See you tomorrow."

Carrie stepped over, and we both watched Greg hustle out of the restaurant. She picked up his plate. "If I didn't know better, I would have said you two must have had a fight."

I wasn't sure we hadn't.

Chapter 7

I pulled out the notebook when I got home. I'd screwed up the conversation with Greg badly and I wanted a chance to fix that one before I talked to my aunt. Who knows, if I didn't, by the time the night was over, I might not have a boyfriend or even any relatives who talked to me anymore. Instead of worrying about what might happen in the future, I decided to worry about what happened to Frank.

Yeah, I know, I told Greg I wasn't investigating, but that was before I also told him that we needed to talk and, somehow, he'd taken that as I was kicking him out. I shook the idea out of my head. He was stressed, I was stressed, it probably hadn't been the best time to open up a conversation about setting up a prenuptial even before he'd asked me to marry him. I paused at that thought. Maybe I was chasing mice here instead of antelopes. But the door had been opened, so I had to tell him what I'd really wanted to talk about so his mind didn't fill in the blanks.

I made a note on my calendar to talk to Greg in the morning, then turned to the notebook. What had I found out since Frank had been killed? I had the description of the truck and the plate number already in my notes. I hadn't asked Greg if that plate had been tracked down yet. So I put a question mark in the margin. Then I added Greg's information about five ex-wives. What did a historical expert make a year? It couldn't be much. I quickly sent my question to Justin via email. As a history professor, he might know. My feeling was, the position wasn't well paid. I put a star by that note and listed off two questions on a second sheet: the one I'd sent to Justin and a second one, how did California deal with alimony now? I'd been out of family law for several years, so things could have changed. And digging into legal work would help me keep my mind off Greg and our minifight.

I went back to the main page. Was there anything else I knew? Then it hit me. Frank had okayed kicking the Mission Wall off the upcoming list of projects to review, but he'd changed his mind and was going to put it back on. That I knew from his own statement to me.

The real question was why he had been so quick to take the wall off the list. And what had changed his mind? Had the wall been part of the motivation behind the killing? Maybe there was someone who didn't want the historical certification of the wall to go through.

Like a developer who wanted to buy the place. Or the mayor, who wanted to get a kickback from the developer? Or Greg, who wanted to set up the area as a barbeque pit? Of course, Greg was off the list because he was, well, Greg. But he'd actually been relieved when I had a reason for Frank to stay alive. Did that mean I wouldn't have been off the list just because I was Jill? I pondered that question some more as I went to the fridge and got out a quart of rocky road.

Relationships. They were as bumpy as a road filled with land mines. Which made me go back to the first question. Who had Frank been married to and what had been the agreements in the divorces? Maybe he'd been widowed five times. He could just have been really unlucky in love. Either way, it was time to do some research.

I keyed in my access to the law library at the local university and started working. Hours later, Emma nudged my leg and I looked up to see that it was already past six p.m. Greg hadn't called or come home, which didn't surprise me, but I thought maybe he might try to clear the air sooner rather than later. I studied the notes I'd made as I'd worked. I'd done a great job in tracking down three of Frank's five marriages. Now I just needed to finish. But first we'd go for a run, then I'd get some real food into me. Again.

I stood and let Emma outside, then ran upstairs to change. As I thought about my plans for the evening, I considered my sugar consumption, especially when I was emotional or stressed. The quart of ice cream had gone down without me even noticing how amazing it tasted. Today I'd run and have a healthy dinner. Even if my love life was rocky. And I would only eat one treat a day. And I needed to enjoy it, not be working on something else and not even notice I was eating.

Pleased with my new resolutions, I finished tying my shoes and ran downstairs. But as I grabbed Emma's leash and a bottle of water, someone knocked on the front door. I set the items down on the entry table and opened the door. A woman stood on my porch and stared at the house like she was measuring square footage. The professional dress and her attention to detail told me all I needed to know. She was a Realtor.

"Good afternoon," She put on a smile that could win a local beauty pageant, if not regionals. She held out a small hand with her nails recently manicured into a bright orange that somehow matched her suit. "I'm SaraBeth Marston and I'm looking for savvy homeowners like you who want to get out from under an older property and into a newer one, where you don't have to worry about the hot water heater. Am I right?"

"Actually, this house isn't for sale." I went to close the door. Now I'd have to wait for her to leave before I could take Emma running. And daylight was burning. Besides, the highway would get crazy crowded with commuter traffic if we didn't leave soon.

"Oh, I must have been informed incorrectly. Are you sure you're not interested in an offer? I have a client who'd pay top money for a cute little cottage like this. And you wouldn't even have to move until the start of next year. They want the deal finalized before next summer." Her eyes gleamed with the potential of a commission, but I only knew of one type of buyer who wouldn't care when I left. A developer. Aaron had sent out someone to do his dirty work for him.

"Again, not for sale, so no, not interested in what the offer might be." This time I met her eyes as I tried to close the door.

"It's really substantial. But I might have caught you at a bad time. May I buy you dinner and we can go over the contract then?"

I shook my head. "You don't listen, do you? I've already said the place wasn't up for sale and you've ignored me every time."

"Think of what that money would do to keep your aunt safe in her golden years. You and Greg could travel the world with what my client is prepared to offer." She made a step toward the door, thinking her talk of money would sway me to the dark side.

I studied her. The girl had done her homework before showing up. But if I thought about it, all she'd have to do is ask a few people about me and my life at Diamond Lille's and she'd probably have this information. Anyway, it didn't matter; I wasn't going to sell.

"I'm going to say this politely one more time. Then I'm going to call the cops. I have two who live right here who'd probably love to talk to someone who's connected with this project. Especially after that poor man was killed so quickly after the developer showed up in South Cove."

SaraBeth held out a card. "I never push. Here's my card. Call me if anything comes up and you want to sell. I'm sure I'll hear from you soon."

"I hope that wasn't a threat." I kept eye contact as I took the card.

The smile came back. "Of course not. I'm just looking out for your best interests." She tried to see inside the house over my shoulder. "People change their minds about selling all the time."

"I won't." I shut the door on her and set the card on the entry table as I picked up the water and Emma's leash.

Through the door, I heard her parting shot. "I wouldn't be so sure."

Locking the door, I grabbed the card and went to boot up my laptop. I let Emma inside, then locked that door as well. While I was waiting for my computer to start up, I went out and watched as she pulled out of the drive in a black suburban. "SELL4U plates. Of course."

Emma whined as she watched me staring out the front window.

I reached down and rubbed her head. "It's okay, girl. Someone just pushed my buttons."

When we got back to the kitchen, I keyed her name into the search engine. Apparently, SaraBeth was a new associate with a small agency out of the city. Probably trying to make a name for herself in commercial real estate, especially if she was working with the developer I'd met earlier that day. Of course, that was just speculation, but it felt right. I reached for my phone to call Greg, but realized he was probably still mad at me. I'd do more research tonight and tell him all about it when we talked in the morning.

He'd probably laugh about the misunderstanding. But something she'd said bothered me. My heart beat a little faster when I realized she'd mentioned my elderly aunt and Greg. She'd either researched me or someone had told her my pressure points. Who was behind SaraBeth's visit? I didn't think Aaron Presley actually knew that much about me, but I could be wrong.

I headed outside for the second run of the day. I only hoped I'd be able to walk tomorrow.

* * * *

Waking the next morning, I was surprisingly free of stiffness. But, I realized, my alarm either hadn't gone off or Greg had turned it off. I didn't have time for a run, so I counted yesterday's second run as my exercise for the day. I wasn't sure it worked that way, but a girl could hope. I showered and got dressed, then hurried downstairs to have a quick breakfast with Greg. I knew exactly how to deal with this. I'd tell him I'd been overanalyzing the situation and he'd totally get it.

But the kitchen was empty when I got there.

I picked up the note and read it aloud as I let Emma out the back. "'Sorry, I had too much on my mind to sleep. I'll call you and we can make plans to talk. Just remember that I love you, no matter what happens. Greg.'"

I set down the note and picked up my phone. We needed to talk, now. The phone rang and Greg's voice came on the speaker. I waited for his voice mail to kick in and started talking. "Look, I don't know what you're thinking, but really, it's not all that bad. I'm just overanalyzing things. You know I do that. And a Realtor came to the door last night about me selling the house. It's got me kind of creeped out. So if you have a minute, call me. I need to hear your voice. Anyway, I, well, I ..." The beep cut off what I was going to say. I debated calling back and finishing the message, but I'd let him make the next move. If he didn't call by lunch, I was going to the station right after my shift and confronting him.

With that part of my day planned, I tucked my notebook and laptop into my tote. Then I let a travel mug of coffee brew while I watched Emma hunting rabbits in the backyard. I liked to leave her out as long as possible on the mornings we didn't run so she didn't go hunting sofa pillows when I left for work. That dog had an addiction.

By the time I got to Coffee, Books, and More, I had expected a few customers waiting outside. Instead, there was a note saying the shop was closed due to extremely high pricing. I ripped off the notice from the door and unlocked it. Steaming, I went directly to the security cameras and replayed the video since the shop closed last night. Greg had insisted I upgrade my security system, and for the first time, I was happy I had.

When I saw the woman come up to the door and tape the notice, I paused the video. It was the artist, Tia. The one who'd patiently explained to me yesterday that she understood my side of the story. "Of all the crappy tricks."

I dialed Greg's number. Voice mail again. So I dialed the nonemergency line to the police station. A man picked up the phone. "South Cove Police, how may I help you?"

"Tim? This is Jill. Look, something happened at the shop, but I don't know if it's a crime or not."

"Jill? What happened? Are you all right? Do I need to come over?" Tim's voice turned from polite to worry. He was a good man.

"Could you? It's kind of hard to explain over the phone, but I don't want to drag you away from anything important."

He laughed. "It's been kind of dead here. I'll lock up the place because I'm alone and be over in a few minutes. Maybe I can snag a cup of coffee when I get there? These night shifts are kicking my butt."

"Of course. I'll have the coffee on when you get here." I hung up the phone before I comprehended what he'd said. He was alone at the station. So wherever Greg had gone last night when he couldn't sleep, it wasn't his office. Had this minor skirmish turned into a full-on battle? I needed to talk to him today before things got totally out of hand.

I went back out front, leaving the video player on the spot showing the culprit. Then I went about my morning routine. I started serving the regulars, and I could pick the ones who hadn't shown this morning. Luckily, from my memory, it looked like I probably had lost only two or three customers today. If they didn't come tomorrow, I'd see if I could reach them to explain the confusion.

One more problem to add to my list of worries. The day wasn't even started and it was turning out to be horrible. I pushed away the negative thoughts. Deek would say I needed to change my aura to bright blue to banish the bad away. I closed my eyes and imagined a circle of bright blue all around me.

"Jill? Are you okay?" Tim's voice interrupted my meditation.

I felt heat bloom on my cheeks. "I'm fine. Just trying to push away the negative energy. You caught me trying out the woo-woo."

"My fiancée does yoga. She's always telling me I need to breathe and find my center." He patted his stomach. "I tell her it's always here. And I haven't lost it yet."

His joke made me laugh, really laugh, and I felt a little of the stress ease away. "Thanks, I needed that."

"So, what happened that you needed some help with?" He glanced around the room. "Doesn't look like vandals. Unless they're the cleaning type."

"Ha, ha." I pushed the paper toward him. "This was on the door when I got here. I'm sure I lost at least three customers this morning."

"Retail warfare? Do you think someone from Lille's is trying to steal your customers?" He took the paper and put it into a plastic evidence bag.

"No. I mean, I don't think so. I think it has to do with the increase in the Business-to-Business dues." When he blinked at me, I realized he didn't know what I was talking about. "Look, the City Council raised the dues the businesses pay to be part of the Business-to-Business group. Well, someone did. Bill is out of town, and he usually is the guy who deals with that area, but while he's out of town, someone's trying to do an end run."

Tim kept nodding. When I stopped talking, he inclined his head toward me. "And…"

"And what?" Now I really wished Greg had picked up his phone.

"I don't get how this would cause someone to be mad at you."

"Oh, yeah. I forgot to tell you that the Council blamed the increase in fees on the high prices we're charging for meeting here and refreshments." Now he wrote something in his notebook. "Okay, that makes sense. Any idea who did it?"

"Yes. And I can also count the number of customers I lost and add that up with their regular order. So I can monetize the damages. You'll need that, right?"

He shrugged. "I guess if the DA decides to file charges, we will. But right now, tell me who you think did this and I can go talk to them."

I pointed to the back room. "I'll do you one better. I'll show you."

After he'd reviewed the tape a few times, he used the keyboard to make and send a digital file to his email, along with Greg's. As he watched, I made a list of the customers I needed to call and what they typically ordered. I made a copy of the list and handed it to Tim. We went back into the main room, where I could watch for any customers.

He put away his notebook.. "I'm going to go down and talk to this Tia. I'm going to tell her to knock it off. If something else happens, let me know, and I'll file charges against her."

"Wait, she gets a hand slap? That's all?"

Tim shrugged. "Honestly, Jill, it looks like a prank to me, and if you put this in front of a jury, they're going to think the same thing. Besides, what did you lose? Nothing except about thirty dollars' worth of coffee sales?"

I sighed. That was really close to the figure I'd determined. Besides, did I really want her to go to jail? "This will stop after you talk to her?"

"This *should* stop after I talk to her. Like I said, if something else happens, call me. Or tell Greg. Either way, we should have it nipped in the bud here." His phone buzzed and he picked up the call. He looked at me. "Hey, boss."

Greg was on the phone. I took a deep breath. This was going to be over and everything was going to be okay. Greg would see to that. I felt stupid, but I whispered, "Tell him that I said hi."

Tim nodded, but he was listening to Greg. "Okay, I'll be right back. Hey, Jill says hi." He paused, listening.

"What did he say?" I sounded like a desperate girlfriend. And I hated that.

Tim squirmed just a bit before he put on a poker face, but I'd seen it. He put away his phone. "He says he'll fill you in later."

I saw the blush as he spoke the words and I realized: Tim was lying to me. If he had to lie to keep my feelings from being hurt, what in the world had Greg said? Keeping up the pretense, I nodded. "I'm sure I'll hear all about it at the dinner table."

Tim pushed out a very relieved-sounding breath. "Great. Well, I've got to go talk to Tia and then get back to the station. I think it's going to be a busy afternoon."

I stared after him for a while, then picked up the phone and called all the customers who'd been stopped by the note. I got answering machines on all the calls, which was just as well. If I'd have to have a real conversation, I might just do what I'd wanted to do for the last few hours. Cry.

Chapter 8

Toby sat waiting at the house when I got home. Sitting outside on the porch with Emma at his side. He waved as I walked up the sidewalk toward him. "What are you doing here? I thought Greg had you on day shift for the duration while he solved this murder?"

He held out a Coke and offered it to me. "I saw you coming, so I ran in to get one. I heard from Tim you had a bad morning."

"Sometimes people can be jerks." I took the soda and popped open the can. Then I took a long swig of the magical concoction. "There's a reason God put sugar on the earth. It's for days like this. I might just eat a quart of ice cream for dinner, unless Greg's planning on being here."

Toby shifted uncomfortably. "He told me to tell you he's going to be working late again. He'll order food delivered to the station."

There were so many answers to that message, but I was going to be an adult and not use my employees as go-betweens. If Greg wanted to, that was his option. I would be the better person. "Okay then, message delivered. You can go back to work."

"Actually, I'm here to talk to you about the real estate woman. Greg asked me to look into her because he said you felt threatened by her." Toby stroked Emma's back, and I swear she was smiling. My dog loved the men in her life.

"Maybe I'm overreacting. She told me I was going to sell the house and she was going to be the one who would list it. She wouldn't take no for an answer." I closed my eyes and took a deep breath. "It's been a crappy week."

Toby pulled me into a hug and patted my back. And the tears fell. "I can't believe I'm crying on your shoulder. I mean, I'm a strong, independent woman. I shouldn't be crying over a pushy salesperson."

"I think you've got more going on in your life than just an in-your-face salesperson. Jackie told me about the Business-to-Business trouble. Tim didn't want to call her. I think he's a little afraid of your aunt. Then Frank died in front of you. And of course, you and Greg…" He took out a handkerchief from his uniform pocket. "Sorry, that was prying. I don't want to know anything about my bosses' fights. It feels like I'm the kid in between two parents."

I took the white handkerchief and wiped my eyes. He hadn't even mentioned the back and forth about the Mission Wall. That had been totally stressful. "I guess it has been a lot. Did Tim talk to this Tia? Did she admit to putting up the sign?"

"She didn't until he threatened to charge her because you had video of her. Then she broke down and said it wasn't her fault. That they made her do the dirty work. Then she promised to leave you and the shop alone."

"'They'? Did she say who 'they' were? If this is a gang, it doesn't matter that she promised; someone else will just take up the gauntlet." I folded the handkerchief. "I'll wash this and get it back to you. Now, I'm going to go take Emma for a run. Unless you have more good news for me."

"This Realtor, do you have her card? I'd like to have Esmeralda run a check on her." He stood to follow me to the door.

"Sure, let me just grab it." I walked inside with Toby and Emma on my heels. The card was sitting on the kitchen table and I handed it over like it was poison. "Here you go; knock yourself out."

He took the card, then tucked it into his pocket where the handkerchief had been. "Don't worry, Jill. Everything is going to work out just fine. You'll be fine."

I watched him leave and wished I had his confidence, his determination. His faith. And I knew the only way to get myself out of these dumps, besides the ice cream sitting in my freezer, calling my name, was to run.

I went upstairs to change, and in just a few minutes, Emma and I were on the beach, smelling the salt air, and I felt my shoulders relaxing for the first time that day. Leaving the beach after my run, I saw two women standing outside their cars in the parking lot. One looked familiar, but the second I knew in a heartbeat. It was Tia. We had come up behind the bathrooms on the edge of the lot. I motioned for Emma to sit, and because she was worn out, she actually followed my command. I could kind of make out the voices.

"I can't do anything more. The police already have their eye on me. If you want to add more pressure, you're going to have to find another flunky." Tia's voice was loud, and her words carried on the early afternoon day.

"I'm not asking you to do anything illegal. Just mess with her some more," the other woman demanded. "My sources say she's ready to break. And the payout will keep you painting those awful pictures for the rest of your life."

Wow, that was harsh. From what I'd seen of her drawing skills, I thought Tia was pretty good. But it was obvious they were talking about me. Who was paying them to upset my life? And the better question was, why? I wanted to go over and confront them, but something held me back. Emma leaned on my leg. She had felt my pull to move and engage too.

"It's over, Mother. If you cut me off, well, I might just have to tell that cute deputy about what's going on."

A door slammed, and I glanced around the building to see Tia's red Mustang peel out from the parking lot, sand kicking up from the tires. The other woman, Tia's mom, apparently, got into her BMW and followed her out of the lot, although at a slower speed.

I glanced down at Emma, who was watching me watch them. "So, what was that all about? Do you want to go home and find out?"

Emma barked her affirmation, but then again, she may have just been saying, *Time for a nap, please.* I'd been pushing her pretty hard the last few days. Maybe we needed to take a day off running tomorrow. I needed to take a trip into Bakerstown to visit the records department at the courthouse to track down Frank's ex-wives.

When I got back to the house, I called Mary.

"South Cove Bed and Breakfast, may I help you?" Mary's voice always sounded cheerful and warm. Like you could sit and tell her your troubles while you ate homemade cookies at her kitchen table. I guess that was why her bed and breakfast was always full and had been featured in a regional travel magazine.

"Hey Mary. I have a question. Actually, two. Any word on when Bill will be back? Has he said anything about the Council letter?" I hated to push the issue, but with the weird stuff going on, this would get at least one issue off my to-do list if Bill could just fix the problem.

"Sorry, Jill, his dad took a turn for the worse and they're at the hospital. I didn't want to bring up Council issues, especially when he feels so bad about not being here to handle the day-to-day work at the bed and breakfast." Mary sighed. "If I don't hear a return date by next Saturday, I'll bring up this whole mess. Maybe he can send Amy a revised letter and have her send it out."

Amy. I hadn't thought of that. I wondered if this Alice had used Amy to send out the original letters. I focused back on the call. Mary sounded tired. "I appreciate whatever you can do. One more question: Do you know anyone who drives a baby-blue BMW?"

"Besides Alice Carroll from the Council?" Mary answered my question with a question. "She has one that has REALTOR plates."

"Wait, Alice Carroll is a Realtor?"

I heard a door close, and then Mary responded, "Sorry, the mail just arrived. Yes, Alice owns her own agency. California Dreaming Real Estate. She has an office near your place. But it's upstairs and doesn't really have a sign. It's over the building the Glass Slipper is in."

Right across the street. Things were either coming together or there were a lot of coincidences going on in South Cove this week. And, somehow, it all focused on my house. "Thanks, Mary. Hey, if you need anything while Bill's gone, give Greg or me a holler. I can send Deek or Toby over to help."

"Aren't you sweet? That man of yours came over first thing this morning to replace a shower head in one of the guest rooms. I called him yesterday because Bill had talked with Greg before he left town. I feel bad for stealing his time from you. But you'll be glad to know he got a good breakfast for his trouble."

"I bet he loved it. But seriously, don't feel bad or put off calling. We're here for you." I was glad Greg was helping out the Sullivans while Bill was out of town, but I had a feeling it was more to keep busy and keep away from me than from his charitable side.

I said my goodbyes and put the information about the note on a page labeled "Targeting CBM?" Then I added all the information I knew about the Council letter, down to Tia's relationship to the woman who'd started the problem in the first place. And what did she mean about the money? Getting Diamond Lille's set up as the official site for the monthly meetings wasn't worth much in monetary enhancements. And from what I knew about Lille, she didn't want the bother of trying to make all the businesses happy. Alice's statement to Tia didn't make any sense. I wrote down the sentence "What about the money?" Then I circled it twice.

I wish I had Greg to bounce these things off, but right now he was too busy solving a murder and helping out Mary. I sighed and closed the notebook. I stared at my dog, who was sleeping in her kitchen dog bed. "Emma, I'm in a mood."

She tapped her tail on the ground, as if to say *it's okay Jill. You deserve ice cream.*

So I got up and started a load of laundry first. Then I grabbed a quart of almond vanilla and took it and a spoon to the living room. Then I put in a well-watched DVD of the first Harry Potter movie and started my marathon.

I only stopped to change discs and heat up a plate filled with chicken tenders for dinner. I'd planned on adding a salad, but it seemed like too much work. I was still on the couch when Greg came in the door at eleven. He greeted Emma while closing and locking the door. Then he came over to the couch and sat down next to me, taking the bag of corn chips from my hand and eating a few.

"What are you still doing up?" He didn't look at me; instead, he started watching the movie and eating my chips.

I sat up and ran my fingers through my hair. "Not sure if I really was awake still. I decided to have a movie marathon and block out the really bad day."

"I heard you had a visitor." He set down the chips and picked up the microwave popcorn bag. He shook it and started eating. I'd only finished about a third of the bag before I'd decided that chips and salsa would be the thing to solve this craving. "And it looks like you've eaten every snack in the house."

"I didn't cook the pizza rolls." *Yet,* I added to the statement. It had seemed like such a chore a few minutes ago when I grabbed the chips. "You heard about the Realtor?"

"I was talking about the note at the shop. Wasn't the Realtor yesterday?" He leaned into the couch and tossed a piece of popcorn to Emma, who promptly caught and swallowed it with one smooth move.

"It's kind of a blur. I made you mad, got the visit from the Realtor who wouldn't take no, and then had the shop thing this morning. Oh, and I watched Tia and Alice fight in the beach parking lot. They said they'd make money if they drove people away from my store."

"And how were they going to do that?" He turned to me, but I'd leaned back my head, and the room was starting to spin. I was bone-tired on a sugar high. The high was beginning to wear off. I had to be at the shop way early before any customer even got out of bed so I could outsmart any message leavers tomorrow.

"I'm not sure. It doesn't make any sense, but nothing this week does." I stared at him with blurry eyes. "I love you, Greg King."

"Now I know you must be sick." He reached out to put his hand on my forehead. I slapped it away from me.

"Seriously, all I wanted to talk about was our future and you pull a crazy disappearing act. Just like the last guy I dated." My eyelids felt doubly heavy now. My focus was slipping, and I knew I'd be asleep sooner rather than later. "Look, I didn't mean anything. I wanted to talk about the house and the Miss Emily account."

"And we will, but for now, close your eyes and go to sleep." He pulled me closer, and I nuzzled his neck.

"I could walk upstairs by myself, but the decision needs to be made now. A couple more minutes of this and I'll be out," I mumbled to his chest.

"It's fine. I'll take care of you."

The next morning, the smell of bacon cooking downstairs told me the encounter hadn't been a dream. I hurried downstairs to see Greg at the stove cooking and Emma lying in her bed, watching him. I opened the door and motioned for her to go outside.

"I already tried that. She went, did her business, then came back to the screen and stood and stared at me. It was creeping me out a little, so I let her inside." Greg poured me coffee and handed me the cup.

I closed the door because Emma hadn't even moved. "She misses you when you're not here."

"I wasn't gone that long. One night I came home, but couldn't sleep, so when I got the text from Mary, I headed over there to work on her shower. She really misses Bill. And I think he's only been out of town a week now." He lifted the bacon out of the pan, then moved it off the burner and turned off the stove. He sat down at the table. "I need to tell you something. Monday was the anniversary of my first wedding. I had been so full of hope. So optimistic. I knew we were going to be together forever."

I wasn't sure why he was telling me this, but with Greg, sometimes you needed the story before he got to the point. "You should feel like that on your wedding day."

"Yeah, but I'd seen the warning signs. Jim tried to talk me out of going to the church that morning. Just take off, he said. I'll give everyone your apologies." Greg shook his head. "Jim never liked Sherry. Not one day when I was dating her. Not one day of our marriage. I should have listened."

"That doesn't bode well for us. Jim doesn't like me either." I really didn't like the way this conversation was going.

Greg chuckled and took my hand. "He doesn't like the thought of us because of his beliefs about marriage. He likes you. He just believes I should have stuck it out with Sherry, no matter what."

"I'm blocking your path to, what, happiness?"

He shook his head. "He knows my path to happiness is right where I am. He even told me last weekend that he's never seen me this happy."

"And yet, he wants you to reconcile with Sherry?"

"Yep. And believe me, the irony of what would happen if I did isn't lost on him. He's conflicted, which I think is a good thing. He's been so busy defending the black and white of the discussion, he never considered the gray. He said to tell you hi when I saw him last Saturday. I don't think I remembered." Greg brought my hand up to his lips and kissed it. "Look, I know I was distant this week and I'm sorry. I was just trying to work through some things."

"About your ex-marriage?" I hadn't considered that Greg wasn't upset over what I'd said.

He leaned back. "Actually, about how I can be different this time around. I want this to be my last marriage when we take the plunge. And I don't want to screw things up like I did before."

"I've been thinking about my past too. I guess Amy's wedding being so close, it's made me really consider what role I had in blowing up my marriage too."

"We really need to learn to communicate better." Greg stood and went to the stove. "Scrambled eggs and bacon okay?"

"Sound heavenly."

Chapter 9

As we ate, I filled him in on what I'd uncovered about Frank's life. "I'm going into Bakerstown to look at the marriage records this afternoon when I get off shift. Do you want to go with me?"

"No, I'm interviewing the first Mrs. Gleason at one. She's been unavailable to talk before this. Said she was taking Frank's death hard." He gave a small piece of bacon to Emma. "Of course, she did have time to call her attorney and have him accompany her to the interview. Did you find any indication of Frank being well off?"

"Money? No, but having an inheritance would explain his being able to work for the historical society. Most of those jobs pay as well as a fast-food joint, without the insurance benefits." I finished the last bite on my plate. "Have you interviewed his coworkers?"

He nodded. "And one of them was kind enough to give us a full application packet when I asked about the Mission Wall. Apparently, Frank didn't have the time to change the status of the project before he was killed."

"I didn't think he did." I narrowed my eyes and gave Greg a hard stare. "You were kidding when you said you were glad I had an alibi, right?"

"You want to be a suspect?" He looked at me, confusion covering his face.

"I want you to believe in me so much, you would never even consider putting me on the suspect list. That's true love." I rinsed my plate and put it and the silverware into the dishwasher. Eating ice cream out of the container for dinner did one amazing thing for cleanup. There wasn't any. Well, except for the spoon.

He came up behind me and put his arms around me. "No, darling. That's not true love. That's being an idiot. I'm going to try to get home for dinner. When will you be back from Bakerstown?"

"Probably about six at the latest. You want me to pick up one of Papa Allen's take-and-bake pizzas?" I filled my travel mug with coffee and packed my tote, grabbing my keys from the wall hook. I didn't have time to walk and get there before the first customer arrived. And I needed to make sure there wasn't another "closed" sign put up.

"That will work. I can't stay long, but I want to talk to you about this Council thing. You shouldn't be getting targeted just because one woman has issues." He walked me to the door. "I'll let Emma out again before I leave."

I reached up and kissed him. Stroking his face, I smiled. "I'm glad you're home. I've missed you."

"Sherry probably wouldn't have noticed me being gone at all. At least not until her credit card shut down." He pulled me into a tight hug. "I missed you too."

I parked behind the building next to Aunt Jackie's car. The windows were dusty, as if it hadn't been driven in a while. Since she and Harrold had gotten back together, they'd been spending a lot of time together. I glanced up at the windows to her apartment. From what I could see, there weren't any lights on, so I would guess that my aunt was probably across town at Harrold's. Because my talk with Greg about the house and the money in the Miss Emily fund had gone so well, I decided to leave well enough alone. If and when they made wedding plans would be soon enough to talk about succession plans for the bookstore, just in case.

I let myself into the store via the back door, turning on lights as I went. I dropped my tote and went into the customer area. I could see the front door from where I stood. No paper plastered on the glass announcing my sins for overcharging the city. But a man stood outside the door, watching the street. I walked up to the door, unlocked it, and then spoke. "Do you need coffee?"

He must have jumped a foot away from me, turning wildly to see who was behind him. "I'm here to see Miss Gardner? The owner?"

"You're speaking to her." Now I was worried. "How can I help you?"

"The city has asked me to do a midterm tax assessment on your building. They are concerned that you've done some major remodeling since you opened and didn't get building permits." He pulled out a piece of paper. "That's my authorization to do a walk-through of the building."

"You have got to be kidding me." I took the paper he shoved into my hand. "I haven't done any major improvements, unless you count cleaning the filth out of this place when we first opened."

"General cleaning isn't usually a reason that would add value." He walked through the dining room. "And the floor and ceiling are original?"

"Since I bought the place. And I don't think the owner before me did any work on the building. It had to be the owner before that if they were replaced."

I watched as he wrote these statements down. "I'll have to do some research, but I think you might have visited just after I bought the place."

"We usually do." He glanced at the doors behind the coffee bar. "That the office?"

"Yes." I glanced at the clock. "Customers will be arriving any minute. Can we move this along?"

"May I look into the office?" He stood and matched my stare. Apparently, he didn't scare easily.

"Of course," I gave in. Either he was going to raise my taxes or not. It wouldn't do to get him angry while he was making the decision. "Can I pour you some coffee?"

"Black in a travel mug will be fine. I need to be back at my office by eight." He went into the office and I heard him move around, open the back door, then close it again. Then he came back out to the front. "I'll send you a letter with my findings, but I'm not sure the woman from the city who called had the correct address. I went through the file last night and I can't see anything that's been put in since our original assessment. The only new appliance that probably cost you some money is that cold box in the back, but it's the same model as before, so I don't think you have anything to worry about."

He took the coffee, thanked me, and left through the front door. A man dressed in shorts and a polo came in after him. "Man, I thought I would be the first one here."

"The tax man cometh..." I waved him closer. "What can I make for you?"

When Deek came in, I checked our tax payments and assessments for the entire time I'd owned the shop. Thank God Aunt Jackie had hired an amazing bookkeeper. She'd even gone through and scanned my records from the time I'd owned the shop before she came into the picture. We'd been stable all that time. The bigger question was, who had called to tell the assessor a big fat fib? I had three guesses and the first two didn't count.

"Do you still have a friend in the county records department?" I had stuffed a new mystery into my tote, just in case I had to wait for access at the county. And for reading material to keep me busy when I got home. Although Greg had been less grumpy about me doing my own brand of investigation on this case.

"Sorry, she went back East for some big government job. I think she's archiving history at the White House." Deek slipped an apron over his head. "Did you need to ask her something? I could call her."

"No, I was just wondering if I could ask her to help me this afternoon. I've got some research to do." I glanced around the shop. I'd done everything from my morning checklist and then some. My aunt was making us sign off for the next person, stating that we'd done our work setting them up. "Give me the clipboard and I'll sign off for my shift."

Deek handed over the purple board. "Your aunt can get intense, man. But then, she does things like buy the whole summer reading program tote bags. That's gold right there."

I signed my name and frowned. "Wait, we have a summer reading program?"

"It starts next month. Each time the kid buys a book, they get a mark on their folder. Once they have ten marks, they get the tote and a free book. It's genius."

And he was right; my aunt did have the marketing gene. Apparently, it skipped a generation, because I didn't have any skill or talent at marketing. I guess maybe my kid might.

"Sounds fun." I waved as I went into the office. "I'll see you tomorrow?"

"Yeah. It's police dude's shift, but he's asked me to fill in. Are you looking up things on the dead Frank dude?"

No use denying it. Deek had the sight. "Yeah, I am. And before you say it, Greg already knows."

"I didn't ask that." Deek's eyes sparkled. "But I'm glad things between you two are better. You looked sad yesterday."

"We're fine." I headed out to my car wondering when my staff had become more than just employees. They were family. I'd run the shop by myself for so many years, it felt weird having people in my life who cared about me and what was happening in my life.

I climbed into the Jeep, turned on the tunes, and headed up Highway 1 to Bakerstown. It was time to put on my research hat again.

As an attorney, I'd spent a lot of time researching cases, finding court documents, and filing the same. But that had been a long time ago, and it felt like another life and another world. I found a friendly clerk who showed me the process for checking the digital records and I started searching for everything I could find on Frank Gleason. It didn't take long to get a hit. And then I had all five marriage certificates. But finding the divorce decrees took longer. The good news was, the marriage certificates gave me a date range that enabled me to narrow my search.

The bad news was, even though I had that qualifier, I hadn't been able to find the last divorce decree before the announcement came over the speakers that the building was closing in ten minutes.

I glanced at my watch. It would take me most of the hour to get back to South Cove, especially in Friday traffic. I tucked my notebook and the copies I'd made and hurried out of the courthouse and to my parked car.

"Imagine running into you here." A male voice sounded to my left, and I looked up into the face of Mike Masters.

"I'm just leaving. Sorry, I have an appointment in South Cove that I'm going to be late for." I climbed into the Jeep and started the engine.

He stepped closer and tapped on the closed window.

Reluctantly, I rolled it down a few inches. If he tried to shove a syringe through the gap, I'd be able to see it. Paranoid, I know, but I'd read it in a book last month. The killer had used the ruse of needing help, then shot the victim up with some sort of narcotic to put her to sleep. My week had been filled with the strange and unusual and I wasn't taking any chances.

He chuckled and leaned closer. "Look, I just wanted to ask if you'd had time to ask your boyfriend about the wall. I know it didn't get fast-tracked for the historical certification, so a mention in my new book might help you get some eyes on that process."

"I'm not sure if I'm comfortable with putting a spotlight on the area. The Castle has to deal with people who don't want to pay the visitor fee and climb over the fence all the time." I knew I was conflicted on the certification. But I figured I'd leave it to the experts. If it was the last remaining part of the original South Cove Mission, it deserved to be protected, even if it messed with my lifestyle.

"I promise I'll let you read, edit, and nix anything you don't want me to say or print. I'm just hopeful that a piece of forgotten history has been found again. And if I can help get your wall certified, I'm happy to help." He slipped a card through the window. "At least let's sit down and talk about the possibility. I'll give you what I've uncovered, and if that doesn't convince you, I'll go away and not write about the wall."

"We're busy for a few days. Let me check with Greg and maybe he can slip you into his schedule sooner rather than later." I tucked the card in my purse, turning away from him for just a second.

I saw a hand with a handkerchief on top and I screamed. Mike jerked back, and I realized the white blur I'd seen had been the card holder he still held in his hand.

"Are you okay?" He reached out his hand to comfort me, but thought better of it and dropped it by his side. "What did you see?"

Shaking my head, I put the car in reverse. "Nothing. I'll call to set up a time when we can talk."

All the way home I thought about what I'd seen. Or what I'd thought I'd seen. I shuddered and decided to put the fake memory away. I needed more sleep and less stress.

When I got to the house, Greg was already there and had burgers out for dinner. He was slicing a tomato in the kitchen and I leaned my head on his shoulder for just a minute. I started to tear up. "Thanks for starting dinner. I didn't mean to be so late. And I forgot the pizza."

"I suspected you got tied up in paper. Research seems to be your favorite pastime. Well, besides reading. And it's kind of the same thing. Besides, I was starving." He turned to kiss me and stared into my face. Setting down the tomato and knife, he wiped his hands and grabbed me by the shoulders. "What the heck happened to you?"

"Nothing. Well, nothing real. It was weird, Greg." I leaned into his chest and took in a deep breath of just Greg. My heart rate calmed and I began to feel less shaky.

He moved me to a chair and eased me down into it. "Tell me what happened."

"I was getting into my car at the courthouse and ran into Mike Masters." When Greg's face didn't show any hint of knowing who I was talking about, I added, "The travel book author?"

"What did he do to you?" Greg demanded.

I shook my head. "Nothing. Get me a glass of iced tea, please?"

Greg stared hard at me, then turned to the fridge. "Go on with your story."

He needed something to do while I talked. I could see his desire to fix this and, from what I could see, there wasn't anything to fix. "Anyway, we were talking and he asked me if I'd talked to you about including the Mission Wall in his next book. When I said no and told him I had to go, he gave me his business card."

Greg set the tea in front of me and sat down next to me. "And that was it?"

"Yeah, except, and this is the weird part, when he handed me his card, I saw a hand with a handkerchief in it. And I smelled something sweet, like chloroform, I guess. What does that smell like anyway?"

"Like ether or a sweet smell." He rubbed the side of his face where his five-o'clock shadow was starting to show. "And you're sure what he really handed you was a business card?"

"Positive. I'd already gotten into the Jeep and had the window cracked just a bit to talk. There was no way he could have put his hand and arm inside to try to put me out. It was just a flash, then it was gone. I was stressed, right? Just seeing things?" I wanted Greg to laugh and ask if I was making this up. Instead, he glanced at his watch.

"Can you finish up getting the burgers ready? I've already seasoned them, and there's a salad in the fridge." He stood and stepped toward the living room.

"Sure, but where are you going?"

He paused in the doorway. "To get your neighbor. I only know one person who deals with visions and sightings. Maybe she can help you work through this."

"So you think I really had a vision?"

He turned away from me but didn't leave the spot. "I got a report of a missing college girl from Bakerstown yesterday. I'm not saying this is connected, but maybe Esmeralda can tell us if you're just stressed or there was something else going on."

I stared after him as he left. This couldn't be happening to me. I didn't believe in Esmeralda's so-called talent or the ability to see into the future or the past. I shivered as I remembered sitting in the Jeep, feeling that fear. A fear I now felt for a completely different reason.

Chapter 10

Esmeralda, dressed in her fortune-teller best, hurried into my kitchen. Satin skirts rustled as she walked, and her white peasant blouse was cinched closed with a black corset. I had to admit, she looked amazing. Her curly hair was loose and bounced as she walked. When she saw me, she stopped dead in her tracks. "Jill, are you okay?"

I'd just finished setting up the fixings for the hamburgers and had washed my hands. I stood facing her, drying them with a towel. "I'm fine. Just a little stressed and overworked."

She shook her head and pointed to a chair. "Sit there. I need to connect with your auras."

Rolling my eyes, I did what I was told. Esmeralda can be a little scary when she's in her psychic medium role. "It really wasn't anything."

"Of course not. Shut up and let me do my thing." Esmeralda sat across from me and took my hands. "Close your eyes and tell me everything from when you first talked to this writer."

I told the story again. This time, I remembered the white blur I'd seen had been Mike's card holder, not the actual business card. I'd already put that away. When I got done with the story, the kitchen was quiet. If Esmeralda hadn't still been holding my hands, I would have thought they'd snuck out the back door, pulling a prank on me.

She released my hands with a sigh. "You can open your eyes."

"So what's the diagnosis, Doc? Am I going crazy? Or growing a third eye?" I smiled at her and took a sip of my tea.

"You joke, but I've always told you that you have the power inside you if you ever decided to let it in. I think, today, it caught some residual energy from a bad situation." She looked at Greg. "The Bakerstown police are looking at the wrong place. The girl was abducted at the courthouse by a man using chloroform."

"I'll have Toby send a tip to the hotline. Anonymously, of course." He picked up his phone. "Anything else?"

"Jill, was the hand from a white guy?"

"White. I thought it was Mike's hand, but it was bigger, I guess. And Mike's hands are manicured and clean. This one was dirty. Like he'd been working on a car or something. You know how grease gets in the cracks?"

I looked at Greg, who was writing things down. "You can't be serious about having Toby call this in. It's a dream. A daydream."

Esmeralda touched my face. "Jill, it wasn't a dream. It was a vision. But it's okay. You don't have to believe. And if it doesn't go anywhere, that's fine. But if it helps the police find this girl, you'd want that, right?"

I nodded, seeing her logic. Calling the hotline wasn't saying that I had a vision. It was giving the police another line of investigation to look for this girl. And if they found her faster, that would be the best for all involved.

"I've got to get back home. I have a client coming in a few minutes." She stopped moving and looked at me. "I'm just across the street if you want to talk more."

"You mean if I'm freaked out and need reassurance?"

Esmeralda smiled. "Or just a cup of coffee and a chat with a friend."

She left the kitchen and Greg followed her. "I'm calling Toby, then I'll be back and we can grill the burgers."

I wondered how Greg could take this all in stride. A message from the other side. Although I desperately hoped the girl that had disappeared wasn't dead. But then, who sent me the vision? Did it work differently when the victim was still alive? And as I got the salad out of the fridge and set the table for dinner, what if it was just the product of my overreactive imagination? I hated to think anyone would waste time on a vision, especially if it had nothing to do with the missing girl.

But if it did, I had to say something. No matter how stupid I felt saying it.

When Greg came back, he grabbed the burgers and paused in the doorway. "Come out and sit with me while I grill. You want a beer or more iced tea?"

"Iced tea is fine." I held up the glass I'd just refilled. "What about you?"

"Grab me a soda. I'm going to go back in after dinner to prep my report for the DA tomorrow." He waited for me to grab our drinks, then held the door as I moved to the back porch. Emma followed and immediately went running to the back of the fence.

"Go get the rabbits," I called after her. When I sat down and deposited the drinks on a small side table, I watched Greg start the grill. "Somedays, I worry she's going to come up on a bobcat or something larger."

"We haven't had a bear sighting in town for a while. But yeah, I worry about her too." He sat next to me. "Tell me about your research. Did you find anything interesting about Frank?"

"Full names of his ex-wives and dates/places of marriages and divorces." I frowned, remembering. "But I'm going to have to go back tomorrow to see if I can get some help. I couldn't find his last divorce paperwork."

"What does that mean?"

I shrugged. "Maybe she filed in a different state, although he lived here, so a copy should have been filed here too. Maybe not. That's why I need some help."

Greg drummed his fingers. "Send me the names. You got farther than I did. I just had the first and third wife's information. Although both of them are sure wife number two's name was Bimbo."

I started laughing. "Caron, if I remember the sequence right. I'll write up what I found and send it to your email tonight after dinner. I guess if you're working, I can do a bit of work too."

He leaned over and kissed my neck. "I'm glad I have someone like you in my life. And I'll make it up to you."

"One of the reasons I love you. You always feel guilty about working too hard, so we get amazing trips out of your guilt spot."

He stood and went to the grill to start the hamburgers. "That's because I know what it's like to have a partner who is less than understanding. You're a gem and I don't want to take that for granted."

We were on thin ice again, talking about our exes, but it felt better than before. The we part felt stronger. So I changed the subject. "I have to finalize the top-three party plans for Amy tomorrow too. It's going to be a busy day. Maybe work will be slow and I can do that in the morning, before my shift ends."

"That sounds good. I talked to Justin, and the guys are doing a bar crawl that night. No preplanning required. Although I'm a little worried about Harrold." He sat down again. "I hope he's up to a night filled with partying."

"I feel the same about Aunt Jackie. The party can't be too crazy, like rock climbing, which I'm sure Amy would love."

He chuckled. "I'm not sure how you'd fare either."

"I could hang. Probably literally. I'd fall my first few feet." I watched Emma as she patrolled the perimeter of the yard. "So you think ax throwing should be out as well?"

"Most definitely." He went to flip the burgers. "These are going to be done quick. What other ideas are on your list?"

I gave him the rundown, and the ones I thought I was going to present to Amy. He nodded and commented in all the right places, but I knew his mind was on the murder investigation. Greg was always thinking.

After dinner, he put away the extra food while I rinsed the dishes for the dishwasher. After we were done, he pulled me into his arms. "Gotta go. I'll be home late."

"I'll be here, sleeping." I kissed him. "I hope you solve this soon. Frank deserves better."

After I typed up the wives' information and sent it to Greg, I pulled out my notebook and looked for holes. I did a Google search on Frank Gleason. Several pictures at high-end charity events with Frank and guest showed up. Or Frank and his spouse. Most of them were with wife number one. Lynda Evans Gleason. From the jewelry and designer duds she wore, I figured she must have come from money. I found an article with one of the pictures and read through it.

"Whoa." I grabbed the link and sent it to Greg. He called me a few minutes later. I didn't even say hello, just started the conversation with, "Did you know that?"

"That Frank was the only child of a multimillionaire, and he managed the family charity trust?" He chuckled. "Lynda didn't mention that. Now I need to track down Frank's attorney to see who's in line to inherit. Thanks for the info and the list. I'm trying to set up interviews for tomorrow. I already canceled my appointment with the DA. I don't have a clue where to even focus my energy. Hopefully, the interviews tomorrow will provide some clarity."

"I just can't believe Frank was rich. He acted like a normal person."

"Just because you come from money doesn't mean you can't be normal," Greg reminded me. "Someone's here. I'll talk to you later. Call me when you turn in."

I set the phone on the coffee table and turned on the movie channel. Thankfully, they were playing an older movie I'd seen and loved. But not too much. I didn't want to get distracted from the internet searching. I finished clicking on all the links for Frank, so then I looked up his charity to see if it had an internet presence. It didn't. I put a note on tomorrow's schedule to look up the annual filings at the courthouse for the charity. It had to file paperwork sometimes.

I also used Google to look up contact information for Lynda. I knew Greg had already interviewed her, but maybe she'd tell a reporter for the

South Cove Gazette more than she would the police. I called the number and wasn't surprised when I didn't get an answer. Grieving widow and all. I left a brief message.

Then I did the same for all the other ex-wives except number five. Emma nudged my foot, and I glanced at the clock. It was already ten. One thing about working the early shift at the coffee house was I also followed the Ben Franklin rule for sleep. *Early to bed and early to rise.* Although the last part of the saying was a little sexist, you had to take into account what life was like back then. So I let my dog out and followed Ben's advice.

Saturday mornings aren't any different for me than a weekday morning. Except Mondays, when I don't have to get up. During the summer we are also open on Sundays, but not early, so typically, Toby picks up the morning and either Nick, once he starts, or Deek, get the second shift. Tomorrow, Toby wasn't going to be able to cover his shift, and Deek had been working every day except Monday, so I didn't want him to have to work both shifts. My aunt took Sunday and Monday off. I didn't want to ask her to fill in. We were getting to the point that we might have to hire another part-time employee, although the only way that would work was if we got someone going to school or just needing a few hours a week. Which meant we had to work around more people's schedules.

Today, I'd work my normal shift, then Deek, and Aunt Jackie would close. If things were slow on Sunday, I could do the weekly accounting follow-up and approve the book order Deek and Aunt Jackie had developed over the last week. Technically, I could add books as well, but they did a great job of covering what we needed.

We didn't have time to run this morning, so I promised Emma a run after I got back from my second trip to Bakerstown that week. I grabbed my shopping list, so if I got done early, I could get that off my Monday list. I might seem like I have a lot of time because I only had to be at the shop for six hours most days, but I was always looking to carve out more time. Especially when I was in the middle of a good book.

I drove to work and parked by my aunt's extremely dusty car. I didn't even have to look up to the apartment; I could feel her absence. I was beginning to miss her. Which was a strange thing to say, especially if you knew my aunt. I opened the back door and realized I hadn't told her about the tax guy who came by the day before.

Hopefully, the pranksters would be quiet today.

I saw the sign on the door when I turned on the lights. Apparently, hope wasn't enough. But because I was early, I probably hadn't missed any customers. I went out to open the door and take down the sign. "Store

Closed Due to Death in the Family." The black letters chilled me to the bone. This was going too far.

I called Greg, and he picked up on the first ring.

"Sorry I wasn't there this morning. I had a call I had to handle." His voice should have soothed me, but it didn't.

"You need to come down to the shop. I have another sign." I hung up, not wanting to explain further. He would see what had me so upset when he got here. I propped the door open and went back in the office for a large sheet of butcher paper we used for story hour and some tape. Then I covered the door, sign and all.

Greg could unwrap it when he came. But I wasn't letting some crazy woman mess with my livelihood. Not anymore.

Coffee was going by the time Greg arrived, and I'd served my first customer, who didn't even ask about the door. He had been too involved in a conversation with someone about a real estate deal that had fallen through. I knew the guy was a flipper from previous conversations, and from what I'd heard, his last attempt to purchase a small oceanside cottage had become a bidding war he'd lost.

He hung up and smiled at me. "You win some, you lose more."

"Isn't that the truth." I handed him his coffee and a bag with a chocolate chip cookie. "On the house today. You look like you need some good karma."

"I think you get the karma. I get the sweets." He held up the bag. "See you tomorrow."

Greg nodded at the man as he left. "You're in a good mood today for the circumstances."

"No one is going to scare me into doing anything. What, they want my house? Or they want the store? Whatever it is, they're sending mixed messages. I can't keep up."

"Maybe it's not related to any of this." He nodded to the coffee. "Can I get a cup while I'm working?"

"Of course." I poured black coffee into a travel mug. "But it is related. At least, Tia's related to Alice."

"What are you talking about?" Greg looked confused.

I put the lid and a sleeve on the cup. "I didn't tell you. Sorry. I overheard Tia talking to Alice Carroll at the beach. Tia told her she wasn't going to do her dirty work anymore and called her 'mother.'"

"I didn't know Alice had any children. That being said, I guess Tia changed her mind." He glanced at the door. "Where's the security feed?"

"I haven't even looked at it." I pointed to the office. "It's back there on the front wall. But it might not be Tia. She seemed pretty firm about not doing it anymore after Toby talked to her. Maybe Alice got a new flunky."

"We'll see. Either way, they aren't smart enough to realize they're being watched." Greg went into the back room, and I poured coffee and packaged up a slice of zucchini bread for a customer.

"Jill? You need to come see this."

I handed the woman her change, then called back. "On my way."

I glanced around; there didn't look like any more customers were heading my way. I walked around the door and glanced up at the monitor for the security system. Greg pushed a button, and the tape started to run. I watched as Deek taped up the sign, patted the door, then left, a girl on his arm.

"Deek did this?" I leaned against the doorway and felt my legs start to give out. "My Deek?"

Chapter 11

I watched the video three more times. It was Deek putting up the sign. Deek, who had betrayed not only Coffee, Books, and More, but Aunt Jackie and me. I pulled out my phone and dialed his number.

"Hello?" His sleepy voice filled my ear. "Wait, is this Jill? How are you? What can I do for you? Do you need me?"

"I need you to stop putting signs on my doors. What were you thinking?" My voice got louder and started to crack. I was going to cry. I knew it. "How could you do this?"

"Wait, what are you talking about? I did what you told me to do. I made the sign and put it up late last night, right after your text. I'm so sorry to hear about your uncle."

I stared at Greg, then handed him the phone. "I can't talk to him. I don't understand what he's saying."

Greg took the phone from me and waved me out into the front area. "Go watch for customers. I'll talk to Deek."

I nodded, not knowing what I was going to do. Deek filled a lot of holes in our schedule. He ran all the book clubs. He even set up our weekly ordering packages. He was an intricate part of our work family and he'd betrayed us. I would never had thought he had it in him.

Greg came out of the back room and handed me back my phone. "Jill, this wasn't Deek."

"I saw him on the tape. What do you mean, it wasn't Deek?"

Greg poured himself a cup of coffee and looked around the empty coffee shop before he spoke. "He got a text from you late last night. You said that Jackie's brother had been in an accident and you'd lost him. You asked Deek to make the sign."

"I didn't text him." I opened the text app and showed Greg. "See? No texts last night at all. And Jackie doesn't have a brother."

"I know. I asked him to send me the number they texted from. Probably a burner phone, but he knows he was played and he feels really bad about it." Greg walked over and took down the sign and threw it and the covering paper away. "No need to test it; we know who wrote it and why."

"Do you think you can find out who texted Deek?" I took a brownie out of the case and took a big bite. I needed food to stomp down the emotions I was feeling. Healthy eating? No, but as long as I could name the emotion, I was okay with it.

"I don't know. But I'll talk to Toby, and you need to bring your aunt into the conversation. If they're using the people around you, there may be more misunderstandings before we find out who is doing this." He leaned down and brushed a bit of brownie off my lips before he kissed me. "Just don't bite Deek's head off when he comes to work. He feels bad enough already."

"As he should." But I smiled to let Greg know I didn't hold Deek responsible. On the other hand, I was getting pretty tired of the games going on. I only knew one thing. If I'd been solid in my decision not to sell the house before, now I was rock solid. No one pushed me out of my house or my town. "I'll see you tonight maybe?"

"Probably. My investigation is stalling out. I need to take some time to think about all this. Maybe it really was just a bad timing hit-and-run." He put a cover on his coffee cup. "Thanks."

"No problem. Thanks for coming out and finding my sign monster."

He chuckled. "I haven't solved that mystery yet. But I will. I think I'll have a chat with Alice Carroll this afternoon."

"Find out when she's sending out the Business-to-Business fee increase retraction letter." I put my empty brownie plate in the sink and eyed the chocolate chip cookie in the display case.

"That will be my first question. Not." He waved as he walked out the door. "Sorry, love, but you're going to have to fight that battle on your own. I'm only in the crime-fighting business."

"Extortion is a crime," I called after him, but I saw him shake his head. Sometimes Greg could be infuriating. I took my cup and my notebook away from the cookie calling my name and sat on the couch. I couldn't eat my way out of this problem. Even though I wanted to. I opened the notebook and made a list of what I wanted to get done today after Deek came in and relieved me.

First up, find that last divorce decree. The county had some issues with misfiling last year, when the local senior agency was setting people up to be scammed. Luckily, the computer experts got that glitch corrected, and from what I'd heard, the new director of the Senior Project was doing amazing work. Paula was a sweet woman and deserved some good news in her life.

And I wanted to stop by the real estate office where this Alice Carroll worked. I needed to get her to stop messing with me and mine before I clocked her one. Okay, so I probably wouldn't really hit her, but I'd want to. Really, really bad. I don't like it when people start messing with my family. Or my business.

I could do the shopping for the week and stock up on frozen meal starters because Greg was going to be working. And I didn't usually buy treats at the store when I had easy access here at the shop.

I wasn't going to run today, I needed to give both Emma and me the day off. But if I got these three things done, then working Sunday wouldn't ruin my weekend. And if Greg was busy tonight, I could get the laundry done while I watched television.

Satisfied with my plan, I grabbed my laptop and started researching wife number one. Lynda Evans Gleason had been in the news since before she started high school. I guess that's what happens when your father is a computer genius. She and her mother attended more charity events than I even thought there were charities. Sometime when she turned twenty, Frank started appearing in the photographs too. They had the longest marriage, according to the records. And they'd both walked away with what they'd owned. No joint assets, according to the overview. How could that be when they were married close to ten years?

I Googled her name, looking for an address, and got a hit. Just down Highway 1 and right on the shore. I wrote it down and decided I'd pop in there before heading to Bakerstown. Probably a dead end, but I could take her cookies from the store as a neighborly gesture. People took food when others died. And I had known Frank. At least a little.

I made notes on the next two wives. Maybe they'd give me more information that could lead to a killer wife down the line.

Deek came into the shop and walked directly up to me. He sat across from me and didn't meet my gaze. "If you want to fire me, I understand. I thought it was you."

"We need a code word. If I tell you to do something out of the ordinary again, you just ask for the code word. Fake Me won't know it." I waited for him to raise his head to meet my eyes. "And no, I'm not firing you. I am tired of someone playing with the shop, though."

"I told Greg everything I knew about the person who texted me. It didn't sound like you, but I thought, given the circumstances, you might just be showing your emotions."

I nodded, considering his statement. But really, I was trying to figure out a cool code word. "American Gods."

"The book?" He glanced toward the paranormal section. We had a larger mythological gods section in fiction now that he had started ordering books. "What about it? I think we have two copies on hand."

"No, our code word. It would be really random and strange for someone to say that in a normal conversation, especially because the book is over ten years old. So you ask me for the code word, and I'll say, 'American Gods.'"

"Maybe it should be 'American Gods rule'?" He shot a smile my way.

I shook my head. "Nope. I like the randomness of the phrase. Just those two words. And I'm sorry they dragged you into this fight."

"No worries. I'll do what I can. And I won't do anything stupid again without your code word." He stood and walked to the coffee bar, stuffing his bag under the counter and putting on an apron.

"I'm heading into Bakerstown. Call me if you need anything."

As I left, a ton of people flooded into the shop from the tour bus that had just stopped down the street. If I'd been a good boss, I would have stayed and helped. But if he got underwater, he could call Aunt Jackie. Besides, he was a big boy. He could handle a tour bus swarm on his own.

I got into my car, and when I reached the highway, I turned left to go find Lynda.

After waiting to be cleared at the entry gate, and then again at the door while a woman dressed in a business pantsuit and wearing a clip on her ear went to see if Lynda was available, I was tired. And I hadn't even got to town yet.

The woman hurried back and waved me inside. "Mrs. Gleason will see you in the parlor. Follow me please. Can I get you something to drink?"

"Iced tea would be awesome." I followed her to a room that looked like it had just been set up for a shot in one of the home and garden magazines. "Showcasing your Style" would be the headline, and there were several unusual items scattered around. There was a journal, the pages weathered and cracked under glass. From what I could read, it was about crossing over the land from St. Louis to here. The wife had wanted to stop in Sacramento and farm, but he kept pushing until they reached the shoreline. Then the husband bought up land. It was that land that the patriarch of the family had parleyed into a large fortune. I wondered how much of the journal was the whitewashed version of the trip, sanitized by years of telling the story.

"My family was one of the original settlers in South Cove. They have written a lot about the Mission that was here back in the day. I hear you and Frank were working on certifying the remains that are set in your backyard." The woman who walked toward me was regal. She held her posture straight and her shoulders back. I'd watched a documentary in which the Queen of Britain walk across a floor just like that. "I'm Lynda. So nice to finally meet you. I order from your bookstore all the time, but I'm afraid I send my assistant to pick up the books. I haven't been out much since my health hasn't been the best." Her gaze dropped to the floor, then she shook her head. "And apparently, I've forgotten how to welcome someone into my home. I'm sorry I was so chatty. Let's sit. Our refreshments should be coming shortly."

As if she'd been waiting for the cue, the woman who'd answered the door came in with two large glasses of iced tea with a sprig of mint sticking out the top of both. She set the tray on a coffee table between us, and there were pink and white macarons on a plate in the middle of the tray. "If there's nothing else, I'll be in the office. Just buzz when you're done and I'll come clear the tray."

The woman watched the other leave. "Martha worries about me. I've been dealing with the family curse, MS, for the last few years. Unfortunately, I'm in the middle of a flare-up, so if I cut this short, I apologize."

"I appreciate you seeing me. I won't take much of your time." I sipped the tea, watching her. "I'm researching Frank and trying to find out why he was killed. When I looked at your divorce decree, I noticed you didn't list assets. I don't mean to be nosy, but you're very well off in that area. Family money?"

"Yes. We both had our trust funds, so there was no reason to argue over money. Frank's was a little smaller than mine; I knew that going into the marriage because Daddy did a full financial audit of his future son-in-law before he'd give permission. He didn't quite live up to my father's expectations, but I was told that although he thought I could do better, he wouldn't forbid it."

She laughed and pointed to me. "You should see your face. Yes, dear, sometimes marriage is more than just a match of chemistry and love. For us, it was combining two dynasties."

"Then why did you divorce?" I picked up a macaroon after I asked that, hoping the cookie would keep those types of questions from popping out.

"Even though we were almost well matched in finances and status, there was no love. No chemistry. We cared for each other, but there needs to be more, correct?"

I couldn't argue that point. I'd seen too many people break up their partnership because of the one missing ingredient. Love.

"Did you stay in touch?" I finished the really amazing macaroon as I watched her.

She shook her head. "Not at first. I was angry he'd fallen in love so fast after we parted. But of course, that rebound never lasts. He'd stop by now and then. Catch me up with his life. I was there when he fell a second and a third time. He really was just looking for a soul mate. But he kept finding people who were more interested in the money. Finally, this last one, I thought she might be the one."

"And yet that marriage ended in divorce too."

She looked at me strangely. "Did it? I hadn't heard that."

Martha came to the door. "Sorry, but your financial adviser is on the phone. He says it's urgent."

"Money matters always are to these people." She stood and reached out her hand. "I'm sorry to cut this short. I enjoyed our time together. You're welcome back anytime. Maybe we could talk about books next time. Being a bookseller must be very exciting."

"Not really exciting, but I love what I do." I reached out my hand and gently shook Lynda's. "I'd love to stop by to talk books. Maybe I could visit in a couple of weeks?"

"Martha will give you her card. Just call, and she'll let you know how I'm doing. Please don't be offended if I'm having a bad day. Life just happens sometimes."

She started to walk out of the room.

"Lynda, do you have any idea who would want Frank dead?"

She stopped and looked me directly in the eye. "I can't imagine anyone wanting that gentle soul out of this world. He made things brighter for so many people. It had to be a random hit-and-run."

I thought about my meeting with Lynda all the way to Bakerstown. What a different version of who Frank Gleason was from the man I'd met and had been frustrated with for years after I'd realized the Mission might have been originally on my property. I'd blamed him for the lack of action on the certification, but maybe he'd been on my side all along.

Not that his support would do any good now. The certification had been a long shot when I'd had a champion working for the agency. Now that he was dead, the fate of the wall was probably dead too. Unless I fought for the certification.

As soon as Greg had solved Frank's murder and this thing with the Council, and Amy's party was over, I was going to sit down with Greg to talk this out. I knew where my heart was leaning. If the wall in my backyard was part of South Cove's origin story, I needed to preserve that. Even if it did make my life less comfortable.

When I arrived at the courthouse parking lot, I thought about the vision I'd had about someone being kidnapped. It took me a minute to settle before I could leave my car. Had I heard about the missing girl before, and my mind just used my own jumble of thoughts to create this vision? If it was true, I hoped my insight would help the police find her before anything bad happened.

My life was too cluttered. I needed to get a few things done and off my worry list.

Step one was to find this last divorce decree. Lynda's words flashed in my head. What if there wasn't a paper trail because they weren't divorced? Where had I heard he'd been divorced five times? Greg had been under that impression too. And he had talked to a lot more people about Frank.

I hurried up the stairs and went to find someone who could make sure I hadn't missed it. I might have just uncovered a clue. Or another dead end. I decided to be positive as I climbed the stairs to the records department.

Chapter 12

Tilly, the most senior of the records clerks, stared at my list again. "There are no records of a divorce between California April Windsor and Frank Gleason. If I had to guess, if there was a divorce going, it probably hadn't been completed. Have you talked to their attorneys? Maybe they changed their minds."

Or maybe this California girl was now really, really wealthy. I gathered my notebooks. "I appreciate you helping me. I thought I must have been missing something, but it sounds like you must be right. The divorce never got filed."

"Sometimes one party tells the other they've filed, hoping the threat will help the reconciliation. Maybe this is one of those times?"

"Could be. I appreciate your help this morning." I tucked everything into my tote. "If you're ever in Coffee, Books, and More over in South Cove, tell them I owe you a coffee."

"I like that place. I make the trip over at least once a quarter to refill my bookshelves. It's a rotating cycle in my house. One book in, two out to the library book sale or the charity box. My apartment's really small." She grinned. "One of the joys of living in paradise, right? High rents."

"Well, I really appreciate the help. I know searching records can be time-consuming." I started thinking about the rest of my to do list as I prepared to leave.

"No trouble. Besides, I'd already done most of the work yesterday, when someone else asked about Frank and his divorces."

"Who asked? Someone from the South Cove Police Department?" I wished Greg would tell me these things, especially when I told him I was researching this. It would have saved me two hours.

"No, she said she was from a law office." She stepped behind her desk. "I thought I had her card here, but I guess I trashed it yesterday when I scanned and sent her the printouts."

"Do you remember her name?" I held my breath.

"Mary, no, something old like that. Martha." Tilly laughed. "I guess my Bible school teacher would be proud of me remembering both Mary and Martha. Although I can't remember what Martha's story was. I guess it's been a while since vacation Bible school."

My mind was still processing that a Martha had been researching Frank. There was only one Martha I knew, and she wasn't from a law office. Was that the reason behind Lynda's cryptic statement about the last wife? I hurried out to my car. I still needed to try to catch Alice to find out why she was torpedoing my shop and my position as the business liaison with the Council.

By the time I got to the Bakerstown office of California Dreaming Real Estate, the place was empty except for a receptionist. I asked where I might find Alice and the girl's eyes rolled.

"Oh my God. She's so popular today. You all know that anyone can sell your house, right?"

Okay, so maybe she wasn't a receptionist. "Someone else came to visit?"

"Some police guy from South Cove. I'd love to get a listing out of there. The real estate prices are amazing, and since the area has become so sought after, I'm sure it would be a bidding war. Especially with the new development going in." She looked at me hopeful. "You don't own property there, do you?"

I decided a solid lie might get me out of the office faster than the truth. "No, sorry. I'm on a committee with Alice, and we need to finalize the next charity event. You aren't interested in buying a table at our trivia night, are you?"

"No. I'm busy that night." She didn't meet my eyes as she took a memo pad from her desk and wrote something on it. She handed the paper to me. "Anyway, Alice is at her other job. She works reception at a law office a few blocks away."

It didn't surprise me that Alice had another job. A lot of locals had two jobs to afford the California lifestyle. But a receptionist at a law firm? That seemed a little clerical for the Alice I knew. "Will she be here tomorrow?"

"She has an open house in the Castle View subdivision." She held out her hand and nodded at the paper. I gave it back, and she wrote another street address on the paper. "There, I think that equals me not buying one of your tables."

I didn't really have a trivia table to sell, so I nodded. "Thanks. And I'll keep this between us."

After I did my grocery shopping, I stopped for a large iced tea at a local drive-in. Then I headed home, trying to put together what I'd learned that day. I needed to get home to write it all down because, right now, nothing made any sense.

When the food was put away, I started a load of laundry and went out to the porch to sit with Emma for a while. I'd refilled my glass with more ice and tea and had my notebook in front of me.

But even after I'd written everything down, a few things didn't make sense. Like why was Martha researching Frank? And what did Alice have to do with the less-than-funny practical jokes being played on my business? I flipped through my notebook and looked at what I'd found out so far. When I landed on Amy's party page, I realized I needed to finish that up and give Amy a few choices. Or we'd be left with whatever choice didn't have a two-week backlog to sign up.

The first suggestion was a class in playing blackjack. They'd provide a dealer, an open bar, and two hours of lessons and open play to get you ready for the casino later that night. The next idea was ax throwing. Not my favorite idea, but within the budget she'd set. The last one was my favorite. We could attend a fifties style stage show with a meet-and-greet preshow with the headliners. None of them were original band members except for the members of some boy band that appeared in one of the beach movies. And, of course, an Elvis impersonator. If we were going to go Vegas, we should go old glam Vegas when it was cheesy and cool.

I wrote out my email, giving her three choices and a deadline. She had until Monday to make the decision; then she could book the adventure. And at the end of the month, we'd be having fun in Vegas.

I put my notebook and laptop away and went inside to make chicken kabobs and barley salad for dinner. As I finished up the prep work, I glanced at today's to-do list, which I kept in a separate notebook.

I marked everything off, except talking to Alice. That one I moved over to tomorrow. I'd stop after my shift at her open house. Maybe I'd get some real answers out of her.

With the kabobs and salad in the fridge marinating, I changed over the laundry. Then I grabbed a book. I was ahead of things even with having to work Sunday. I could take the rest of the afternoon to read. And I knew just the place to do it.

I dragged out a chair and my book and refilled my iced tea glass. Then I locked the front door and headed out to the backyard and my secret garden.

Greg found me there three hours later. I'd almost finished the book and I was in a story haze. My tea was gone and I needed to visit the restroom. Greg had a beer and a chair.

"I'll be right back." I kissed him and ran to the house. Emma stayed with him.

When I came back, I'd grabbed my own bottle and my notebook. I pointed to his beer. "You off the clock tonight?"

"I'm hoping so. I told Toby not to call me unless aliens land on the City Hall lawn." He glanced at the bottle. "I figure I can have one now and one with dinner without having a problem."

I told him what I'd made for dinner, and he grunted. Not the rousing *yes* I'd expected, but sometimes he didn't like new dishes, and this barley salad was one I hadn't made before. I set my book aside. There would be time to finish it later. "So, I talked to the first Mrs. Gleason today."

"She's interesting. I did my interview earlier. She was all shock and saddened in the right places, but there was something else I couldn't put my finger on. What did you get?" He sat on the stone wall, setting his beer next to him. Something I figured he wouldn't be able to do if the wall was ever certified. I decided to hold that conversation for another day.

"She was too up front. They didn't have the spark. They both are, were, independently wealthy and it wasn't enough." I sipped my beer. "She was hurt, blah, blah, but it's all better in the end. And I almost bought it, except for one thing."

He grinned. "Okay Columbo, what's the one thing?"

"Her assistant was doing some research at the county courthouse. Or, actually, had a clerk do the research on Frank and his many wives. She was sent the information yesterday. And I don't think the assistant does anything without the first Mrs. Gleason's approval."

"That is interesting." He paused for a minute, and I could see him checking out this new information with the theory building in his head. "What about the latest one? What did you find out on the divorce?"

"Nothing. California April Windsor Gleason still seems to be married to Frank. I sure hope she goes by Cali. Can you imagine naming a kid after a state?"

Greg chuckled. "So Alaska James King is out for our firstborn?"

"Definitely. Especially if she's a girl." I smiled at the thought. I knew he was teasing me, but talking about baby names just seemed right for this soft April afternoon. "Have you found her yet?"

"Not a sign. She has an apartment in the city, but according to her landlord, he hasn't seen her for a week or so. Her rent got paid at the first by electronic transfer, but I had him do a welfare check and no one's in the apartment. No clothes gone that he could tell, no suitcases missing. It's like she vanished. But then again, he's was her landlord. Maybe he didn't know everything she owned." He rubbed his face. "I put in a missing person report with the locals, but who knows how long she's been gone?"

"What about her job? Maybe they know something."

"Cali was an up-and-coming artist, according to her landlord. And yes, she shortened her name. She'd even had her first show last month." He rolled his shoulders. "The apartment complex is filled with writer and artist types. The guy who owns the building screened applicants carefully and gave the creative types a substantial discount for their rent. Or he did before."

"Before what?" I asked the question, but I had a sinking feeling I knew the answer. "The building was Frank's, wasn't it?"

"Yep. Apparently, that's how he met the last Mrs. Gleason." He opened his notebook. "Frank owned an apartment building down in the city in the neighborhood with all those galleries Jackie and Mary like to visit. The building manager—who's working on a novel, by the way—told me that Frank sent out notices to all the art schools in the area about cheap apartments. The occupancy rate is nearly one hundred percent all the time. When an artist hits it big and starts making enough to live on, he's invited to leave."

"Isn't that an interesting word choice. Not evicted, but not welcome. Kind of like low-income housing for the creatives." I glanced at my watch. "Do you want to see what we can find out about Cali while I grill dinner?"

"You want me to keep working while I'm home? That's not part of the bargain. I'll grill and you do your Google research."

As we walked back to the house, Greg carrying the chair for me, I thought of something. "But if she was married to Frank, she wouldn't qualify to live there. Right?"

"The manager didn't know anything about any marriage. He said he suspected she and Frank were dating, but they kept it very quiet around the building." He set the chair on the porch. "Interesting, don't you think?"

"Frank is more interesting dead than I realized he was alive. I thought he was just a jerk. Now I wonder what else he was doing with his money to make the world a better place." We went inside, and Greg went to the fridge to grab the kabobs. I grabbed my laptop.

"Have you Googled Frank besides his wives? I mean, I looked at his charity events, but I thought he was attending those because of Lynda." Greg paused before he went out to the porch to start the grill. "I'm going to have to dig more into Frank's financial life than I'd expected at first glance."

I typed in the shortened version of Cali's name and waited to see what came up. I didn't have to wait long. There were a lot of hits on her recent show. Some of her works were highlighted. Kind of a mix of modern art and Renaissance work. One was a picture of the beach, but with my coffee food truck on the side. Fireworks went off in the distance. A piece of South Cove's history. I bookmarked the page and decided to buy it for the store if it wasn't already sold. Of course, with the artist missing, I might not be able to purchase the painting.

Greg came back inside, and I showed him what I'd found. Which wasn't much. He studied the picture I'd found. "She has a nice eye for bringing the scene to life. It feels like you could just walk onto the beach."

"Yeah. I'm going to try to buy it."

He looked at me funny. "Did you see the price tag?"

"It's only a few hundred. I'll buy it for the store." I shut down the computer. It wasn't the time to be talking about finances. "So, how was your day?"

He didn't miss a beat. If the purchase had made him uncomfortable at all, he hid it well. "Busy. I'm beginning to believe that the easiest answer to Frank's death is the correct one. A random hit-and-run."

"So no leads at all?"

He shrugged. "None that look better or worse than any of the others. I'm intrigued by this missing wife lead, though. Maybe that will pan out to be something. I appreciate your help with the research there."

"Any time." My tone must have held a bit too much excitement at the thought of helping Greg with future investigations because he laughed and stood, squeezing my shoulder as he walked by.

"Don't get too comfortable here. You know I'm not thrilled with you poking your nose into these investigations. People die. Other people are killers. This isn't a book." He slipped out onto the porch.

"I know it's not a book, because then I could skip to the end and find the killer." The window was open, so I knew he could hear me. But maybe he wasn't paying attention. I stood and closed my laptop. Then I reached for the plates. "Although that is cheating, and I rarely do that."

"Rarely as in never, or rarely as in always, but you don't want me to think badly of you for skipping ahead?" He came back inside to get a platter.

"I plead the fifth." I took the salad out of the fridge, as well as a fruit bowl I'd made earlier. I'd also picked up a loaf of fresh French bread at the store, so I put that on the table with butter. We had chocolate chip cookies for dessert. As I waited for Greg to bring in the kabobs, I surveyed the spread. Not meat and potatoes, but a good dinner nonetheless. At least I thought so.

"And here's the star of the meal." Greg set the platter in the middle of the table, then pointed to Emma's bed. "Go lie down. You know you're not getting anything tonight."

Emma looked at me for support, but I shook my head. "Sorry, girl, no human food. You have dog food in the mudroom."

Instead of heading to the mudroom, Emma plopped on her bed and stared at us, hunger filling her eyes.

"She looks pitiful, like we never feed her." Greg laughed and then sat down. "This looks great, Jill. Thanks."

Surprised, I smiled and sat next to him. "Thanks. I wasn't sure you'd approve."

"Any meal I don't have to plan or think about is all right with me." He squeezed my hand. "I appreciate you."

"That's nice to know." I felt warm and loved. I was about to reciprocate with a long kiss, but a knock on the front door interrupted us.

He stood and glanced at the kabobs. "At least it's portable."

"Don't jinx us. It's just a salesman. Or Esmeralda wanting to borrow a cup of sugar." I moved the platter closer to the middle of the table. I didn't want Emma to think that the fact we had walked away meant she could help herself. I stood at the edge of the kitchen so I could see both the door and the table. Emma put her head between her front paws.

I had a bad feeling about our visitor.

Chapter 13

When Greg opened the door at first, I couldn't see anyone; then he stepped back and Mike Masters walked into our living room. He smiled and waved at me. I returned to the table and moved the food onto the cabinet and the kabobs into the microwave. They just might stay warm if our uninvited guest didn't stay too long. I filled a fresh glass with iced tea and took it and mine out to the living room. "Greg, this is the writer I was telling you about. Mike Masters. Mike, how do you like your tea?"

"Black is fine. Thank you." He reached out and shook Greg's hand. "Look, I know you all have been busy here, what with Frank's death and all, but I wanted to talk to you again about the Mission Wall. We don't want a piece of California history to be forgotten for centuries again. The wall waited for years to be found, and when you took the steps to preserve it, that meant something."

Greg motioned to the chair and the iced tea I'd set down in front of it. "It meant Jill's been put in limbo for the last four or five years. That's all. Sit down, Mr. Masters. We'll hear you out, but ultimately, it's Jill's house and her decision."

Mike sat and sipped his tea. "This is good. I've been grabbing one at the shop before I start my afternoon writing session. Your barista is a real character."

"Deek has his moments." I sat down next to Greg on the couch. "Look, I'm not sure I'm refiling the application."

"Don't tell me you're selling to that developer!" Mike set down the glass on the coaster a little too hard. "A piece of history is worth a lot more to South Cove than a water park."

"I didn't say I was selling to anyone. And how do you know about the developer?" I leaned forward, watching his reaction.

"I'm a writer. I watch everything. I overhear people talking." He squirmed a little in the chair.

When Greg raised an eyebrow, Mike blushed. "Okay, so I eavesdrop. It's not illegal."

"Illegal, no, but it's rude." Greg didn't move from his spot. He had his arm draped casually around the couch. He looked relaxed, but I'd taken a body language class. For men, taking up as much space as possible was a power move.

"I'll agree with that. I just hate to see guys like that win. They come into these small towns, promise the moon, and when the parks don't make money, they leave. And the park falls apart with disuse. They're like those frackers in the west. All they want is the money. When the money runs out, they're gone." He took another sip of his tea.

"I said I wasn't selling. In fact, I've told everyone I'm not selling." I glanced at Greg. "They can't make me sell, right? I mean, the mayor had been pressuring Miss Emily to sell, but that was because of the way she kept up the place. Now the lawn's all green and I've painted the house."

"No, honey, they can't make you sell." Greg squeezed my shoulder. Then he focused on Mike. "Look, I get it. You want to include the wall in your next book. If we get anxious about the city trying to push this on us—I mean, on Jill—she might be more agreeable to letting you include the story. But they aren't going to intimidate anyone, not in my town. And neither are you."

Mike held up his hands. "I'm not the bad guy here. I'm trying to help. Look, I heard the developer talking to his girlfriend. He said that the process is working and he should have this deal sealed up in a few days. I don't know what process he was talking about, but I think the two of you should be careful. These guys mean business."

Greg and I exchanged a look. If the developer was behind my issues at the store, it also meant that Alice Carroll might be in with the developer. This all had started just a few days ago. Frank had tried to warn me about something. "Wait, how did you know he was talking to his girlfriend?"

"I was at the county records place, looking up land deals. I heard Aaron Presley talking on the phone to someone, and man, they were hot and heavy. I figured it was a girlfriend and not a wife, because it was the fun, flirty stuff you do at the beginning of a relationship, you know?" He blushed again. "Then he said he'd be back in the city sooner than he'd expected because things were going really well."

"Did you hear her name?" I leaned forward again, hoping that he'd say Alice. If she and the developer were having an affair, I could use that to get her kicked off the Council. I already knew she'd used Tia to do some of the dirty work. Even if the mayor hated me, he wouldn't stand for these kinds of shenanigans. That was his area of expertise.

"No, yes, maybe." Mike shrugged and held up his hands. "I don't know. He had all kinds of pet names for her. Baby, honey, sweetheart. And something else, but I can't remember. It was a couple of days ago, and I was trying to hear if he'd say anything about the development. I wanted to have something solid to bring when I came to talk to you."

"Well, if that's all, we're done for tonight. Jill has dinner waiting for us and I hate to let food grow cold." Greg stood. "We have your number. As soon as she makes a decision, she'll call."

Mike popped up out of the chair. "I promise the write-up will be glowing and fair. And I'll let you read the section before I send it to my editor."

"I haven't said yes yet," I reminded him as he shook first Greg's hand and then mine.

"I know, and I appreciate you hearing me out. I think it's important to have a dialogue about how we honor the past and those that have gone before, don't you?" He moved toward the door, still chatting. When he got outside on the porch, he paused and looked at the house. "It would be a shame for anything to happen to such a lovely house."

We watched him leave and then went inside, Greg locking the door and the deadbolt before following me into the kitchen. I reset the table and didn't look at him when I asked him the question that had been haunting me. "Did that sound like a threat?"

Greg hugged me. "Nothing is going to happen to your house or your shop. Not on my watch."

As I got out the kabobs and filled my plate, I wondered if he could really stand behind that promise. Or if it was just wishful thinking.

After dinner, Greg helped me clean up the kitchen. He leaned over and kissed me. "Sorry to do this, but I'm going into the office to check some emails and do some research. Something Mike said earlier has me twitching a bit."

"And you're not going to tell me." I dried my hands on a towel. "No biggie; I have a book to read anyway."

Tomorrow was going to be a busy day without Toby, and I really wanted to get to the end of the story. I was curled up on the swing on the back deck, my iced tea almost all gone next to me, when the phone rang. I glanced at the display and put down the book before I answered.

"Hey, Aunt Jackie, what's going on?" I hoped it wasn't anything with the shop. I really couldn't deal with another issue right now.

"I'm just closing up the shop and wanted to talk to you about this Vegas trip at the end of the month." I heard clatter as she moved cups from the dishwasher and back on the shelves.

"What about it? I sent Amy three suggestions. Don't tell me she hated all of them and didn't want to tell me directly." I really didn't want to go back into researching a new venue for Amy's party. When I mark something off my to-do list, I like it to stay marked off.

"What? No. I mean, she didn't say anything to me. What in the world did you suggest?"

I ignored her question. "So, if it's not about Amy's party, why are you calling?"

"Well, Harrold and I want to take you and Greg out to eat while we're there. So don't make any plans for Sunday."

"Oh, well, that's nice of you. You know you don't have to do that." I didn't think my aunt had ever offered to buy me a meal before. Aunt Jackie thought eating out was too much work. Probably because she'd worked in the restaurant business for so many years, she didn't see the draw. Then a thought occurred to me. "Are we going to one of the famous-chef restaurants? Like Emeril's?"

My aunt laughed. "Maybe. Just keep the day free for us, okay. And don't forget to tell Greg. I don't want him stuck on a blackjack table and not remember."

"I don't even know if Greg plays blackjack." The phone buzzed in my ear. My aunt had hung up on me. "That's strange."

"I leave you alone for a couple of hours and you're getting strange phone calls?" Greg came out of the house with two beers. He handed me a bottle. "I thought we'd have a drink before we turn in. I think we should celebrate the fact that Toby never called."

"The night is young." I took the bottle and took a sip. Greg moved my book to the table and sat by me. "No, that was my aunt. She wants to take you and me out during our Vegas trip."

"One of the celebrity chef places?" Greg nodded his head. "That would be awesome. I wonder if your aunt knows someone."

"That was my thought at first, though she's being really cryptic about it." I leaned my head on his shoulder. "Do you play blackjack?"

"I do. Do you want to learn while we're there?"

I could feel his breath on the top of my head. "How do you know I don't know how to play?"

"You told me a few years ago. When I was playing with a group of guys from Bakerstown PD. I invited you to come, and you about laughed yourself off the couch." He picked up Emma's ball from the deck floor and threw it out into the yard. Emma took off after it. "So why did you ask?"

I felt my shoulders raise. "No reason. Just something she said. So anyway, keep Sunday free that weekend. I'm sure she'll have us going to the early bird seating so she can save money."

"Sunday is all about you and your aunt. Got it." He took the drool-soaked ball from Emma and threw it again. Then he wiped his hand on a towel we kept outside just for this reason.

"And Harrold. He'll be coming along too."

I saw the smile cover Greg's face before he leaned back into the swing. "I wouldn't doubt it. I really like the two of them together again. I can't believe your aunt thought she could get away with dumping him. He's perfect for her. And almost as stubborn."

"I'm sure you're not saying that people in our family are stubborn."

He chuckled and pulled me close. "I like my life. I don't say stupid things."

* * * *

Saturday morning, I get to sleep in an hour later. We open the shop a little later because no one wants coffee at five in the morning on a Saturday. At least not people who don't have to be up to get to their city job. I had time to run with Emma, and by the time we were back, Greg was up and working in the kitchen. He had made coffee, and a bag of doughnuts from Lille's sat on the table.

"You realize I run to keep off the calories from these things." I held up a maple bar from the bag and took a large bite. "I'm on a vicious cycle. I eat, therefore I run, so I can eat, so I run."

"That's why I'm so glad they opened the gym in the station. I can sneak in a quick workout in between meetings or first thing in the morning when I get there." He closed his laptop. And took out an apple fritter. "I don't mind working out if it means I can eat more of these."

"You know you're supporting a stereotype." I poured myself a cup of coffee and leaned against the counter. I needed to get upstairs to shower, but I wanted to stay in the kitchen and chat with Greg.

"Someone has to." He grinned and held up the doughnut. "Long live the doughnut. May it always be the breakfast of champions."

"Dork." I finished my maple bar and sipped my coffee. "You working here today?"

He shook his head. "Nope. I'm going into the station. I'll see you after your shift. When do you get off, one?"

"Probably, if Deek's not slammed. At least he doesn't have any book club meetings this week." I drained the last of the coffee from my cup and put it in the sink. "See you later."

"Call me if something's hinky about the store." He paused and started to stand. "On second thought, maybe I should walk in with you."

I put a hand on his shoulder and eased him back into the chair. "There's no way I'm letting anyone scare me into changing who and what I am. I get it, they want me to sell. I'm not going to. Case closed."

"For you maybe. Honey, think about it. They've already killed one person." He stared at me. His aqua-blue eyes seemed troubled.

Holding up a hand, I recited a pledge. "I promise I will stay on the sidewalk, look both ways before crossing the street, and run like a banshee is after me if I see a car on the road."

He smiled and returned his attention to the laptop. "I get it, you're a big girl. But seriously, if something happened at the shop, call me. I might be able to get some traceable evidence this time. I have a feeling you're ticking them off."

I paused at the bottom of the stairs. "Why do you say that?"

"Because I'm about ready to strangle you, myself." He waved a hand, dismissing me. "Go to work. I'm trying to research here."

For all my bravado with Greg, I did feel a little exposed walking to the shop. No one was out and about due to the early hour. Tourists like sleeping in on their vacation, and I appreciated the thought process. Heck, I wanted to sleep in and I lived here. When I arrived at the coffee shop, there were no signs papering the door. The café tables in the front weren't damaged or thrown through the front display window. The place looked surprisingly normal. I took a deep breath. Maybe the hazing had ended.

The doors unlocked and the coffee brewing, I was ready for my first customer of the day. It took an hour before anyone showed up. Which wasn't unusual for a Saturday. When the first person arrived, I was going through the Advanced Reader Copies the publishers had sent that week to see what the next book I was going to read would be.

I'd narrowed it down to a self-help book about setting goals for women and a horror novel from my favorite horror guy's now-writing son. I heard the bell go off over the front door and set both books down on the desk to save them from being picked up by another staff member. Then I went back out to the shop, my mind on the books behind me.

A woman stood at the counter waiting for me. As I approached, I realized it was Alice Carroll. I stopped forward movement and wondered what the heck I was supposed to say. Yesterday, I'd been primed to talk to the woman, but I didn't like it when anyone brought the fight directly to me. Gathering up my courage, I willed my feet to move. "Good morning, welcome to Coffee, Books, and More. What can I get for you?

Alice turned to me, and from the lines on her face, I estimated her age to be late fifties to early sixties. Her blond hair was cut into a swinging bob and her lipstick was way too red for her skin coloring. But what drew me in was her deep blue eyes. Eyes with fire behind them.

"I'll take a large coffee." She pulled out her wallet as I stared. Tapping her card on the counter, she arched one eyebrow. "Do you need to ring me up before you pour?"

"What? No, I mean, one large coffee. A to-go cup?" My hand hovered over the cups, waiting for an answer.

"To-go is fine. I've got an open house soon. I need to get going." Alice scrolled through her phone while she waited for me.

I poured the coffee and rang up the charge. "That will be four dollars and seventeen cents."

She handed me her credit card.

I needed to say something. To ask her what she thought she was doing. And ask her why she thought she could just come in for a coffee when she was trying to torpedo my business. As I tried to phrase the opening in a diplomatic way, I ran her card.

"Hey, Jill." Deek bounced into the store. "I scheduled the middle school book club early and forgot to tell you. They should be arriving anytime."

I pushed the pen and charge slip across the counter with her card. This was definitely not the place to have this conversation. I'd stop by the open house, even if it was her turf in battle strategies. I was hoping this would be more of a conversation and not a battle. "Thanks for coming in."

"Make sure that house is spotless when I get there. The last one I did for that builder had been the workman's lunchroom for what had to be months." Alice turned away from me, and it took a minute for me to realize she was talking into an earpiece, not to me. I'd been dismissed as soon as I'd poured the coffee.

After she left, Deek watched the doorway. "That woman's aura is jet-black. I think you should stay away from her."

I nodded and didn't mention to my psychic barista that I was planning on ambushing her later that afternoon.

In a deserted house.

Sometimes my planning sucked.

Chapter 14

Deek's only book club of the day kept us busy right up to the time when I was supposed to leave. I'd told him before it started to let me know if he thought he'd need me to stay later, but he'd brushed it off. "That's why I moved this one up a couple of hours. I wanted to get it done before you left. Did you see how many books those kids bought? They put me to shame."

"They're off on summer vacation. What else is there to do but read?" I checked the treat case. I'd just finished restocking it a few minutes ago. The place was clean, again, and the last of the kids, with their parents, had left the store.

Deek sank onto a stool in front of the counter. He drank down a glass of water. "Man, I love those guys, but they have so much energy."

"You're working a lot of hours, especially since Toby bailed on us this week. Do I need to hire someone else?" I studied next week's work schedule, which Aunt Jackie had put up last night. Toby had three shifts, but I wasn't sure he'd be done working overtime with Greg by then.

Deek shrugged. "I only have two classes this semester and they're almost over. I'm not taking classes this summer and Nick will be back, right? I can probably hang on until either he's here or Toby's hours at the station are cut."

"And when are you going to write the great American novel?" I made a mental note to talk to Aunt Jackie soon about maybe taking on another part-time person. We had a budget meeting a few days before we took off for Amy's party. With both her and me going to Vegas for a weekend, we might have to hire a temp for a week anyway.

"I'm writing. Here and there. I get a few words at school, then more here if it's slow, then a few at night when I can't sleep. It all adds up." He rolled his shoulders. "I have no idea if it's any good or even making sense, but I'm loving the story. And I guess I'm my first reader anyway."

"When do you think you might start the writing group here? Did you ever talk to Jackie?" I'd forgotten and hadn't mentioned it to her, but then again, Deek had the idea. He needed to promote it.

"I wrote a proposal and sent it to her last night. She said we'd talk at the staff meeting at the end of the month." He grinned. "Not sure if that's a good thing, but it's out in the world."

The bell over the door rang, and an attractive woman in her midtwenties strolled in. She glanced around the shop like it was the Hogwarts Castle in one of the amusement parks. Her black hair was tied back in several braids and she wore a yellow sundress. I labeled her a tourist and smiled at her when her gaze met mine. Something about her looked familiar, but I couldn't figure out why. "Can I get you something to drink while you're looking around? We carry a wide variety of books, from beach reads to best sellers to local historical fiction."

"A mocha would be awesome." She nodded at the table. "I see you have Wi-Fi. Do you mind if I hang around a bit and check my email?"

"Of course not." I nodded to Deek. "We'll get out your mocha and you can pay when you're ready. Deek will be glad to answer any questions you might have. I'm out of here."

Deek came around the corner of the coffee bar. "Go have fun. If I need you, I have my phone."

"Sorry it's going to be a long shift. I'll be available if you need me to come back." I saw Greg coming up the sidewalk. "Maybe I should just stay?"

"I think I can handle one customer. I promise if an unscheduled tour bus comes into town, I'll call." He finished the mocha and put whipped cream on the top. "Go, spend time with Police Dude. He looks a little worn out."

I studied Greg's face as he walked inside the shop. Deek was right; Greg did look tired. I thought the lack of progress on Frank's murder must be wearing him down. Of course, having the stuff going on at the shop probably didn't help. We needed a real vacation, not just a weekend away to Vegas for Amy's party. "Call me if you need me."

I met Greg just a few feet away from the door. "Can I buy you lunch?"

He nodded. "Then I've got to go back to the station. Wives number two and three are coming in for interviews. They couldn't get off work during the week."

"Then let's have lunch and we can talk about anything but the case or my shop issues." I linked my arm in his.

"There are other subjects besides crime, murder, and intimidation? I think you're joking, right?" He squeezed my shoulders.

"Of course. We can talk about how I need to hire someone else part time. Know of anyone who doesn't work for you who needs a job?"

We left the shop and walked slowly down to Diamond Lille's. It was a beautiful spring day, and I was surprised that we didn't have more tourists sharing the streets. Maybe people were still getting their yards ready for the upcoming summer or watching their kids play Little League. It was funny what made a good weekend into a terrible one for sales. And what took a terrible one for the weather into an amazing sales weekend. I'd given up trying to guess what type of day the shop would have. Although since Deek had started the extra book clubs, I'd seen an uptick in both book and coffee sales on a weekly basis.

The store would be fine. As soon as I got Alice Carroll off our backs.

Diamond Lille's was packed, and as if I'd called her up by thinking her name, Alice Carroll stood at the hostess stand. Lille was staring at her, and I tried not to laugh at the look the diner's owner was giving the woman.

"All I'm saying is, it wouldn't kill you to have an actual keto menu. It's the in thing now with all the celebrities."

"Good for them." Lille stared at her nails, which today were painted a goth black. She glanced at us, then sighed. "Let me go to the kitchen to see if your order's ready yet."

I thought she was showing tremendous self-restraint by not adding the rest of the sentence, which was something like *so I can get you out of my face.*

Greg must have seen my intentions as he grabbed my arm. I shook loose, then approached Alice. "You're Alice Carroll, right?"

She was focused on her phone. "That's me."

"The Realtor?"

That got her attention. She changed her face from totally bored to a welcoming smile. Until she saw me. I swore I saw fear flit across her features for a second, then it was gone. "You're Jill from the coffee shop."

"Yeah. I can't believe we haven't met before. Well, besides when you came in for coffee this morning. Did you get your open house done?" I knew how to do small talk. I just didn't like it.

Alice laughed, but it seemed faked. "I'm on my lunch break. I get exactly ten minutes to pick up food, and I have to pray the perfect customer doesn't come in when I have my associate watching the house. Otherwise, my commission is cut in half, just because it takes this place so long to get food out."

"Oh, good. I was planning on stopping by this afternoon. I had hoped we could have a short chat." I froze my gaze on her. "About the local real estate market?"

"Are you thinking of selling?" A sly smile made her face look dangerous and not friendly at all.

"See, that's the thing. Someone has been spreading a rumor about my house being for sale. I wanted to find out what you knew about the problem." I nodded to Carrie. "Sorry, that's our signal. Our table's ready and I'm starving. I'll stop by later and we can continue this conversation."

"I really don't know anything…" Alice called after us, but I ignored her.

When we got settled and I had my food ordered and a vanilla milkshake on the table, I leaned back in the booth and relaxed.

"Do you want to tell me what that was about?" Greg was watching me. Alice had left a few minutes after we'd walked away, but had shot daggers at us in that short amount of time.

"Basically, I'm letting her know that she's the one messing with me and I wasn't going to let her do that anymore." I sipped the shake. Heaven.

"You think that was what she heard?" He watched me with the shake.

I shrugged. "At worst, she knows I suspect her. And she'll be nervous all afternoon about what I'm going to ask her."

"Don't tell me you're actually going over there."

Carrie dropped off our food. "Thanks," we both said in unison, not meeting her gaze.

"Okay then, I won't interrupt the conversation." Carrie laughed and left the table.

"I haven't decided. If I thought she'd be even half honest with me, I might. But I think I did what I needed to do. I put seeds of doubt in her plan. And if she knows that I know it's her, maybe she'll leave the store alone." I picked up the taco burger and bit into it. It wasn't the healthiest lunch, but I'd had a few bad days.

"You might be playing with fire." He focused on his own food. "But then again, you may have just solved your issue. I don't speak female very well."

"You translate just fine. I'm not sure she'll take the hint, but at least she knows that I know she's behind it. And that's half the battle. You can't be a political figure and not know how the games are played. And I think she's a shrewd player."

"Because she waited for Bill to leave to start?"

"That, and using her daughter and Deek to actually do the dirty work. I bet that Realtor who came to my door works for her agency. She's just moving around the chess pieces, but not putting herself, the queen, in play."

When Greg didn't say anything, I glanced at his face. "What? I've been reading a chess mystery. Those players really know strategy."

Lille approached our table. "Food good?"

"As always." Greg smiled at her. "Tiny is a genius in the kitchen."

She nodded, then looked at me. "I heard from Harrold that you've been having problems at the shop. I wanted to let you know that I'm sorry about your trouble. People just need to learn how to be nice. It wouldn't kill anyone."

"Thanks." I was shocked at the sentiment. Lille hated me, or so I thought. But she loved Harrold. Maybe that was moving me off the bottom of her list and into her good graces.

"Well, enjoy your meal." She moved away from the table.

We stared at each other for a full minute. "Did that really just happen?"

He shrugged, watching Lille yell at a server for letting the food sit in the warmer too long. "All I can say is, it has to be the power of Harrold. He tames the most ferocious of female creatures. Lille, your aunt..."

"Hey." I started to say that my aunt wasn't that bad, but Greg was right. Aunt Jackie could be a complete bear if she wanted to be. I realized I hadn't seen her in a while and decided to give her a call this afternoon. She was off the schedule for the weekend; maybe we could sit and talk for a while. "You could be right."

Greg changed the subject. "So, when is Bill supposed to be back? How's his father? Should we do something?"

"You already fixed the shower in their bathroom. I think Mary appreciated that more than just sending flowers. I'll call her this afternoon to see how she's doing." Another reason I missed talking to my aunt. I didn't get any of the local gossip. Amy was too busy with the wedding. Sasha used to be my finger on the pulse of the community, but she moved away to the city for an amazing job offer. The store got cards from her every once in a while. I was happy and proud of her accomplishments, but that didn't mean I didn't miss her.

"There is a lot going on this week, isn't there?" Greg glanced around the crowded diner. "People go on with their lives with chaos all around them. And if you don't pay attention, things happen that you can't fix."

"You can't take care of everyone, Greg." I could see that Frank's investigation was weighing on him. Probably harder than any he'd worked on before.

"It's not that. It's just trying to keep in touch with the people who mean something to me. I haven't talked to Jim in over a month. And my mom has to call me for us to stay in touch. I need to be better at keeping people close." He smiled at me. "Like you do. You probably talk to your aunt every day. And Amy. And Sadie. You keep in touch with your friends."

"Well, not so much this week. I was just thinking I needed to reach out to Aunt Jackie because I haven't talked to her for more than a few minutes lately. Even about this shop stuff." I finished my lunch. "So, I guess we're both slacking in the friends and family category."

"At least we're keeping tabs on each other." Greg reached over and squeezed my hand. "I've got to go to work. Please tell me you're not going over to this open house to confront Alice. I'd like to keep seeing my girlfriend and not have another murder to solve."

"Well, at least we'd know the killer in this scenario." I finished off my shake, but from the look on Greg's face, he wasn't amused. "Don't freak. I won't go over there. I was kind of thinking it was a bad idea anyway. And I need to stay close to the phone, just in case Deek needs me at the store. So, I guess it's housework day."

"You promise?"

I ate a stray fry that had hidden behind my coleslaw container. "I promise. Although I might do more reading than cleaning."

"As long as you're home and the doors are locked, I don't care. Esmeralda has clients this afternoon, so if you're in trouble, call her. She'll come over until I can get there." He pulled out his wallet and threw cash down on the table for the meal. Greg was old-fashioned. Every Friday when he got paid, he took out cash for his meals out. I would have used my debit card, but he said it helped keep him accountable. When he was out of cash, he stopped eating meals out. The good news was, he got paid every week.

I grabbed my tote and followed him outside. I took his hands and reached up on my tippy-toes to kiss him. "I promise I'll stay safe."

"You better change that to try to stay safe. You have issues even when you're on your best behavior." He touched my cheek. "Do you need me to walk home with you?"

"I think I know the way." I squeezed his hand. "See you tonight for dinner."

"Meat and potatoes, right?"

I laughed. "I'm not trying out any recipes, if that's what you mean."

As I walked the sidewalk toward home, my thoughts were on Alice and her reaction. She knew something about my house and the problems I'd been having. I had proof of that. Now I just had to keep her scared of me so she'd stop playing her games.

I paused at the door to Harrold's train shop. His son was behind the counter, and he waved at me as he saw me in the window. Maybe I wouldn't call my aunt. It looked like she and Harrold were off doing something. I didn't want to interrupt them.

I kept walking, but when I reached the alleyway that ran behind the train shop and Diamond Lille's, I heard voices. Maybe Aunt Jackie and Harrold were just now leaving. I looked around the corner, but instead of my aunt, Alice Carroll was standing in the alleyway, talking to a guy in a large black Ram. The truck had the same license plate as the one I'd called in. It was the truck that had killed Frank. The one Greg had been unable to find.

I ducked back around the building and ran into Harrold's store. I ran behind the counter and sat on the floor. Herman, Harrold's son, stared at me. I pulled out my phone and called Greg. "Hey, Herman. If anyone comes in, I'm not here, okay?"

"Sure, whatever you want." He didn't look convinced, but I was almost positive he wouldn't tell Alice I was hiding behind the counter.

The phone kept ringing, and finally, Greg's voice came on the line. It was his voice mail.

I called again. I'd give his cell one more try, then I'd call 911. The guy who killed Frank was right behind the building. We had to catch them. And I couldn't walk home until Greg did just that.

Chapter 15

This time, Greg answered the call. "Hey, Jill, I've got an issue to take care of here at Josh's. He's had a break-in."

"The truck that hit Frank is in the alley behind Harrold's and Diamond Lille's. And Alice is talking to the driver." I think my news saw his break-in and upped the ante with a murder. Yes, the cards reference was from another book I was reading.

"Where are you?"

"On the floor in the Train Station." I looked at Herman, who'd turned white.

"Tell Harrold to go lock the door and put up the closed sign. Then the both of you get into the back."

"It's Herman, not Harrold." I put my hand over the mouthpiece and relayed the information to the shaken Herman.

"Just close the store."

I nodded. "Lock the door and close the store. As soon as Greg comes, you'll be able to reopen."

He walked over and locked the door, turning the sign to "Sorry We Missed You." And instead of screaming in terror to the back room, he paused at the counter. "Now what?"

"You call 911 and I'll follow you into the back room. Lock that door too." I didn't know there was a door, but there was one in my shop, and our buildings seemed to be built in the same manner.

As we made our way to the back room, I heard a key turn in the lock. Turning, I saw Harrold and Aunt Jackie walk in the front door.

"What in the heck is that kid doing?" Harrold grumbled. "This is prime walk-in time and he's got the door locked."

"Maybe he ran to Lille's to pick up food," Aunt Jackie suggested. "You shouldn't be so hard on him. Besides, we'll have to wait for him to get back before we can move some of the heavier stuff up to your apartment. I don't want you doing that on your own."

I popped up and ran to the door, pushing my aunt and Harrold out of the way and toward the back room. "Go get in the back. Greg's on his way."

"What are you talking about? Why are you locking the door again?" Harrold took my aunt's arm and moved her to the back room. At least he wasn't fighting me as if he questioned my sanity.

I clicked the lock and glanced out the window. No one was standing there with a gun. Which was a good thing. "I'll tell you when we get to the back. I didn't see your car out front. Where did you park?"

"I have Herman's truck and I parked it in the alley by the back door. I can't leave it there long; your boyfriend will ticket me." Harrold pointed to one of the chairs near the desk. "Jackie, go sit down, and Jill, tell me why we're hiding on a sunny Saturday."

"Was there anyone in the alley when you parked there?" I knew the answer from Harrold's look.

"No. It was empty. Why?"

I went to the window. An older green Chevy sat by the door. The black truck, and probably Alice, were long gone. "Then we don't have to be back here."

A knock on the front door confirmed my statement, and Greg stood there with Toby. I went over and unlocked the door. "I swear, they were there just a few minutes ago."

"I believe you. I'm going to go back to the station to review the security tapes from this street as soon as I've checked on you." He reached out a hand and shook Harrold's, then Herman's. "I haven't seen you in a few days."

"Jackie's been keeping me busy. We were going to wait to tell you two tomorrow over dinner, but you kind of caught us red-handed." Harrold put his arm around Jackie. "We're shacking up."

Aunt Jackie slapped his stomach. "Now, Harrold, don't call it that. We are being sensible. We've been spending so much time together, it just made sense."

I pressed my lips together, trying not to laugh. I glanced at Herman. "I guess the kids are the last to know."

He shrugged, grinning. "I knew this morning when Pops called to borrow my truck and my muscles. So, I guess *you're* the last to know."

Toby laughed, but when I looked at him, he turned it into a cough. "Well, if everything's all right here, I'll go back to Josh's and finish the break-in report. Weird thing is, nothing seems to have been taken. But the back door was clearly kicked in."

I sent a quick glance to Greg. In the back alley, it was hard to see what door led to what shop. Had they just mistaken Josh's place right next door to mine?

He put a hand on my shoulder. "Look, I'm sure it's a coincidence."

"Maybe, but maybe that's why I didn't get hit last night. They damaged the wrong door."

Toby paused on his way out. "Man, I'm not telling Josh that. He'd be mad at you."

"I know. He'd probably think I needed to pay for his damage because it was my fault he got hit." Things were crap right now. With a capital C.

My aunt stepped closer to Harrold. "Jill, maybe we should talk about what's been going on. I think you've kept me out of the loop long enough."

"Well, get your moving done and come on over. I'll be home the rest of the day and after one tomorrow. Deek and I are splitting the Sunday shifts."

Toby looked sheepish. "I could come in. I have a few hours before I have to go back on nights."

"And when are you going to sleep? We're fine, although Jackie and I need to talk about hiring someone else." I made waving motions with my hand. "Go take care of Josh. You know how worked up he can get. You're on the schedule for Tuesday, Wednesday, and Thursday next week. Let me know if you can't make it."

As he walked out, Greg kissed the top of my head. "Thanks for making him feel better. He's getting closer to full time with me, but I'm sure he'll want to keep a few shifts for his house fund."

"And another one bites the dust." I looked over at Herman. "You're not looking for part-time work, are you?"

He laughed. "I have a full-time job that actually pays enough to live on. Sorry, Jill, but I'll ask around."

"I might know someone." My aunt looked thoughtful. "I hadn't thought of hiring someone now, especially with Nick coming home soon."

"I'm not sure Nick is going to want to work. According to Sadie, he's already interviewing for full-time spots in the city. The kid's a powerhouse. And she hinted that he was taking a trip to Europe this summer too." I rolled my shoulders. "The life of a small business in a small town. We're always hiring."

Harrold shook his head. "I just cut my hours. I haven't had anyone work with me except for Herman, here, for years."

"And you barely make enough to pay the building costs." Aunt Jackie looked around the showroom. "I was going to wait until we were married, but it might be time to think about either expanding or closing."

Harrold looked down at her, shocked. "Close the shop? Then what would I do with my time?"

"And that's our clue to leave. Let me know if you all are planning to come to dinner over at Jill's tomorrow. I'll make sure I set up my day so I can make it." Greg led me to the front, then paused at the edge of the alley. "So, you saw the black truck and Alice? Anything or anyone else?"

"No, I'm sure it was the truck because I checked the license plate. And we'd just seen Alice at Lille's." I didn't remember seeing a driver, but I hadn't taken a lot of time to stare. "I should have gotten closer."

"You did exactly what you needed to do. Got somewhere safe and called me. Actually, I'm kind of proud of you. I can't believe you finally listened and stayed away from danger." He pointed to his car on the other side of the street. "I'm parked there."

"And?" I didn't understand his point.

He put his hand on the small of my back. "I'm dropping you off at home. You're not walking anywhere until I find this truck and its driver. You need to stay safe."

"I'm not an idiot." But I followed him to the truck and crossed over to the passenger side. I'd accept the ride home because I wanted to. No use being all principled and freaking out whenever I saw a vehicle coming my way. Besides, I just wanted to lock myself in the house and watch movies. Ones where I knew the ending and everything would be okay. And maybe some ice cream.

"Okay, didn't mean to insult you, but if you're letting me drive you home, I'm fine with that." He started the truck. "So, your aunt and Harrold are moving in together. How are you feeling about that?"

"After the whole breakup thing, I'm not looking a gift horse in the mouth. They're good together and they both deserve to be happy again." I watched out the window. "I guess I have an apartment to rent. I wonder if Toby wants to upgrade his digs."

Greg chuckled. "I'll mention it to him, but I think he likes the money he's saving by living in a studio. Do you want to make up flyers? I can post them down at the station."

"Not just yet. Aunt Jackie thought she knew someone, but that might have been for the job. I don't know, everything's so crazy right now. If that falls through, then yeah. I'd rather have someone living in the apartment so that the building isn't completely empty once the shop closes." I turned and studied him. "Do you think Josh's break-in was actually meant for my shop?"

"Maybe." He ran a hand through his hair. "Okay, probably. There just wasn't any rhyme or reason for it to be Josh's place. He had money in the till. Small, valuable antiques in the display case that would have been easy to access and take. But nothing was touched. It was like they got in and realized they were in the wrong place, so they left."

"Good thing I installed the extra security. Do you think they know I put up the cameras?"

Greg stared at me. "I'm an idiot."

"Okay, I'll bite. Of course, you are. But what are you talking about?" I got my keys out of my tote. Emma wasn't going to be happy we weren't running, but she'd get over it. Especially when I had an afternoon of cuddling on the couch planned.

"Your cameras cover that entire back parking area. I bet you got something on your feed. I'll call Toby and have him go over and check it out." He pulled the truck into the driveway, then leaned over and kissed me. "Thank you for what you did today."

"Freaking out Herman and calling in backups for a truck that wasn't there when you got there?" I rested my hand on the door lever.

"For thinking about calling me first. And keeping yourself safe. Sometimes you barge in where you shouldn't."

I shrugged. "I knew what he did to Frank. I wasn't taking any chances. But I'm really going to give Alice a piece of my mind if we're right about her. I can't believe someone would do all this over a land deal."

"If that's what's happening." Greg laughed at the look I gave him. "Okay, so it looks like Alice is knee-deep in this, but looks can be deceiving. We need to prove she's involved."

"In the movies, she'd be locked in your cell at the station already." I climbed out of the truck and walked around to the driver's side. "Thanks for the ride."

He kissed me. "I'll wait until you're inside. Please lock the doors. I'll call when I'm heading home. And in the movies, the first guy or gal I locked up would just be a red herring and the real killer would be hiding in your house."

I shivered and glance at the porch. "Don't say things like that. Maybe you should come in and walk through."

"You're fine. I was joking. Besides, you have Emma. She's not going to let anyone in besides the people she trusts." He leaned back in his seat. "But if she doesn't greet you, back right out. I'll be watching."

"Great, now I'm scared of my own house." I tried to joke it off, but Greg did have me a little worried.

"You should be cautious. Someone is messing with you and someone else is dead. It might be total coincidence, but you can never be too careful."

When I opened the door, Emma stood there, tail wagging. I waved at Greg and went inside, locking the door after me. "Hey, sweetheart. Do you need to go outside?"

The dash to the back door answered my question. Emma was house-trained, but even she had her limits. And I'd been gone a while. I followed her into the kitchen, picking up the mail from the floor as I went. A pink envelope with familiar handwriting caught my eye.

I sat at the table while Emma explored the backyard and opened the card. It was from Sasha. A picture of her, her daughter Olivia, and a tall, black man at Disneyland fell out. Everyone was smiling, including Minnie Mouse, who knelt by Olivia. I turned to the card.

Just wanted to let you know Olivia loved the gift you sent for her birthday. She wore the South Cove T-shirt to Disneyland. Michael took us for the weekend. He works for a hedge fund here in the city and is supersmart, especially with numbers. We're happy here, safe, and making new friends, but Olivia and I miss our South Cove family. Tell everyone we said hello.

I studied the picture again. Sasha had moved on. I'd thought that maybe after the internship, she'd come home and patch things up with Toby, but I guessed this Michael was the new man in her life. I let Emma inside, locking the kitchen door, then put the card and letter away in my office. From what I could see, Toby wasn't even dating yet. His heart was broken. Seeing Sasha and Olivia happy with another man in the picture would just be cruel.

With my newly imposed house arrest, all I could think of doing were outside things. The flower garden I needed to plant. The swing that called to me to come sit and read. Instead, I grabbed an iced tea and my research notebook and turned on the television to the cooking channel. I wasn't looking for new recipes, but the shows in the background were calming and helped me focus.

As I saw it, the first ex-Mrs. Gleason was a strong front-runner on the list of possible killers. Even with her physical limitations, she had the money to hire out a hit-and-run. And she'd had her assistant researching Frank's marital history. I wrote down all the "facts" I thought made her look guilty, then, after the research item, I wrote one word. Why? Why was she so interested in Frank's love life now?

I turned the page and wrote down everything I knew about Alice Carroll. I didn't really have any evidence that she was involved in Frank's murder except for the last item. She'd been seen with the murdering truck. Well, I'd seen her with the truck. Hopefully, one of the security cameras had picked up this image as well. I hoped Greg would find it.

Then I made a page for the last wife. California. Where was she? Was she just on some artist retreat or was something more sinister involved in her disappearance? I wondered what Frank's will said. Who got the family money he'd been living off and donating during his lifetime?

I gave the true history author his own page, but he didn't have any reasons to want Frank dead. In fact, from what I could see, he was on the same mission as Frank. Save and make people aware of the disappearing California historical sites before they were all torn down and replaced by water parks.

That line of thinking made me write down one more suspect. The water park developer, Aaron Presley. He had reason to get rid of Frank if he was truly working on getting the wall in my backyard certified. If I had a historical marker, they couldn't buy the property and flatten the land for a parking lot.

I glanced around the living room I'd painted myself right after I'd inherited the house. This place was home now. And no amount of money was going to change that.

I picked up my phone and made a call to the Heritage Society. Because it was Saturday, I only got voice mail, which verified their hours as Monday to Friday, eight to five. I put a note on my calendar to go visit them on Monday.

I wanted to see exactly who was taking over Frank's caseload and look at the file for the wall. Then I could decide if it was worth my time to start over.

I closed the notebook and picked up the remote. Scrolling through the channels, it didn't take me long to find a rerun of a sappy movie. Emma moved from the floor to the couch and laid her head on my lap. And we stayed there until Greg got home a few hours later.

Chapter 16

Sunday, I didn't have a customer for two hours after I'd opened. No one had tried to break in. Or plastered the front windows with paper. Or tried to con an employee into closing the shop. I sipped a hot chocolate as I glanced around the clean and empty shop. I probably should have cut hours today without Toby, but we'd make it through. And because nothing had happened to the shop, I wondered if the pranksters had taken a day of rest. Or if my talk with Alice had actually made her think twice.

I didn't care what Greg said about proof. I knew Alice was behind all the problems I'd been having lately. I started to wonder what I could do to her real estate business for payback. Cancel ads in the paper? Call up sellers and tell them the company was going out of business? Spray-paint her sidewalk? The last one held some merit, but then I decided the sugar was getting the best of me. I needed to play a clean karma game here, even if she didn't.

Sometimes being the bigger person in the argument didn't feel as satisfying.

A couple wandered in and I made some drink suggestions. They waved me off and went straight for the bookshelves. My kind of people. I moved from the couch to back behind the coffee bar. The author speaker notebook was tucked under the bar. I opened it to this month and saw a new entry in Deek's neat printing script. Mike Masters had scheduled a book talk and signing for next Thursday. The guy was persistent, that was for sure. I couldn't be mad at Deek. Masters was an author and in the area. Deek had probably thought he'd hit the nail on the head with this event.

I realized the couple was waiting in front of the counter. A large pile of books sat in two stacks, and from the titles, it looked like a his and hers division. I picked up the top book from what I assumed was her pile. "I loved this book. She's really clear about steps to achieve financial freedom. Even with starting in debt."

"I've heard great things about it, so I told Nan I'd buy it for her." He glanced at the menu. "Can we get two large iced teas to go? That would be awesome."

I made the teas, then rang up the purchases. "Anything else? All our bakery items are fresh this morning and tasty."

"Well…" She started, but he gave her a look and handed me his credit card.

"We don't eat sugar." He took one of the teas and handed it to the woman.

"Clive, we are on vacation." She took the glass, but her attention was on the chocolate chip cookie display on the top of the case. "One cookie isn't going to hurt."

"It's a slippery slope, Nan." He nodded at me. "We're done."

I ran the card and handed the slip and a pen to him. I felt like giving her a cookie, but figured he'd just throw it away. I didn't want to be controlled like that. Not in a marriage or in any type of relationship. I thought again about Frank and his wives. Why had his marriages dissolved? Lynda had said they'd just fallen out of love. Or, no, she said they'd never been *in* love. Would he make the same mistake over and over? Or did he make mistakes with people while he was looking for love?

Deek came into the shop a few hours later, and I was still thinking about the no-sugar couple. He lifted his hands and held them out. "Whoa, your aura is dark, like you're in pain. Anything I can help with? Do you need to leave early?"

I shook my head. We had several customers hanging out in different spots of the shop, but no one needed my attention right now. I leaned over the counter. "I just had an encounter with a husband and wife that were stuck in the fifties. Why would people try to control another person like that?"

Deek came around and tucked his bag under the counter, getting ready for his shift. "People do all sorts of things to one another. And a lot of the time, they don't realize what it does to themselves. Angry words, controlling actions; it's all because people are insecure. At least that's what my psych professor claimed in our class last week."

"It could be worse, I guess. They just got me in a funk." I pulled out a cookie and ate it for the woman whose husband wouldn't let her have one.

"Emotional abuse is still abuse." Deek shook his head. "Some of the clients' who visit my mom's salon come in to try to talk to their dead husbands. They don't know what to do with themselves without someone telling them what to do. It's sad really."

"If you were an artist and you took off from your apartment, where would you go?" I decided to change the subject. This one was getting way too dark. "For a day or longer?" His face looked thoughtful. "And where is their apartment?"

"Does it make a difference?"

He nodded. "It does if you want me to give you a good answer."

Was he using his sight for this? "She lived in the city. Near the art gallery neighborhood."

He opened his computer. "Let's check out that area. If she lived there, she probably doesn't have a car. That's mostly a walking neighborhood."

"And parking cars is expensive in the city." Now I was curious. I watched as he opened up the Maps section of his browser and nailed down the neighborhood. I pointed to a building near one of my aunt's favorite. "According to Greg, she lived in that building."

He put a virtual pin on the building, then zoomed into the area. "Nice place. Probably has a doorman. Did Greg talk to them? Maybe she had a car come for her or asked for a taxi?"

"Good questions." I took out my notebook and started writing down questions. "What else do you know about the area?"

He zoomed out and pointed to a train station. "The commuter train doesn't even have a stop in that area. She'd have to walk ten more blocks to get to the closest station. Did she take bags with her? If so, that's a long way to walk with a suitcase. Someone might notice her. I'm betting on the cab/car thing. Unless she didn't go willingly."

My mind flashed to the idea of someone putting a cloth over my mouth. The vision had been so real that day. Could it really have been a sign from Cali? Greg had thought the source had been a missing girl who had been reported out of Bakerstown a few days ago, but we hadn't known that the fifth wife was in the wind then.

I put down the pen and took a cup, filling it with coffee. I really didn't want this. I liked being normal and not "seeing" other things. Esmeralda had warned me that I was a natural sensitive. But knowing the right door to open was a lot different from feeling someone else's fear. I sipped the coffee and watched Deek study his laptop.

"It's not all bad, you know." He didn't look at me. He stayed focused on the screen. "Sometimes you get ideas that help others. That's the best. I'm not like my mom, but I guess her gift filtered down to me in my ability to read others. You have something there, I'm just not sure what."

"According to Esmeralda, I'm good at reading others too." I sipped my coffee. "But this isn't about me. This is about a missing woman. Any other clues you get from the area? That was a good call to look at the neighborhood. Maybe you should think of a career in law enforcement."

He laughed. "Me? A police dude? I'm not in to all those rules and stuff. Besides, I know my calling now. It took a while, but I think this author path is the one I'm meant to be on. I'm really digging telling this story. My mom's worried that I'm going to be a poor artist for the rest of my life, but I've got plans. It's going to be all right."

I wasn't sure if he was talking about his future or if the last sentence had been aimed at me and my fear of what was going on with me. But I didn't want to get into that kind of a discussion now. "You'll be a great storyteller."

The doorbell went off and a couple walked into the shop. He called out a greeting, then closed the laptop. "Let me think about this some more. I know some people who are in the art world. Maybe they know this chick. Can you give me a name?"

I gave him Cali's full name and he shook his head. "Parents can do a number on their kids."

The couple moved toward the bookshelves, and I moved to greet them. Deek put a hand on my arm. "Why don't you head home? I can handle this for the rest of the day. If I need help, I'll call, but you look beat."

I felt beat. Usually, I'm up and excited for the day. Today, I had to drag myself out of bed. "Are you sure? I haven't done the shift change list yet."

"Your aunt will never know. I didn't finish one this week just to see if she'd notice, and she told me what a great job I'd been doing. Hanging out with the Harrold dude has been good for her."

"I can't disagree there." I glanced upward at the soon-to-be-empty apartment. "I might have an apartment to rent soon if you're interested."

"Unless it comes free as part of the job, I'm not. I'm trying to save for a writer's retreat this fall in Colorado. Mom's fine with helping me with tuition, but she sees this as extracurricular." He glanced over to the couple who were still focused on the books. "I might know someone, though."

"Hopefully, renting this won't be as hard as I'd expected." I took off my apron. "I'm going to take you up on your offer and head home."

After yesterday's warning from Greg, I'd driven the Jeep into work and parked it in the back. The parking lot looked empty without my aunt's car sitting in its usual spot. I guess I'd just have to get used to the fact that she was living her life. Usually, it's the adults who get empty nest syndrome, not the kids. But then again, I guessed I was an adult now. Which made me even more depressed. Time to go home and veg on the couch until Greg got home.

Or it would be after I sent him a list of Deek's questions and ideas. I briefly thought about just driving into the city and doing my own research, but if Greg found out, especially after the warning he'd given me yesterday, I would be sharing the doghouse with Emma.

Not that my spoiled dog even used the doghouse Greg had built her a few summers ago.

I thought about Frank's murder, the offers on the house, and the attacks on the store. Were they all related? If that was true, there was one person who could be tied to all of it. Alice Carroll. I wished Greg could just arrest her based on my intuition, but I guessed the Constitution gave even suspects as guilty looking as Alice some rights.

When I got home, I realized I hadn't asked Deek about Mike Master's signing. Not that I'd nix it now. Or, I guess, ever, but I wondered how it came up. Had Deek suggested it, which was my hope? Or had Mike thought it another way to get in my good graces? If he knew how much work an author signing could be, he would have told Deek no and really been in my good graces. Just another sign I wasn't a good bookstore manager. I loved the early shift. A few customers to keep it interesting, fresh coffee and treats, and plenty of time to fall into a book. Which reminded me, I'd told Deek that I'd have my book recommendation for the newsletter in by Friday. And I hadn't even chosen the book I was going to recommend. There were so many good choices in this month's new releases.

I decided I'd work on that this afternoon. Right after I emailed Greg. At the house, I reached into my purse for the house keys. My phone was vibrating. Crap, I'd turned it on silent mode last night so I could get some sleep and hadn't changed it back. Amy was calling. "Hey."

"Hey? That's all you got? Where are you?"

"I just got off work and pulled up at the house. Why? Where are you?" I put my tote over my shoulder and made my way to the front door. Emma had heard me pull up and was already barking.

"Well, I'm not at Diamond Lille's waiting for you anymore. I must have called ten times. Why didn't you pick up? And why were you at work?"

Uh oh, I'd forgotten about my weekly brunch with Amy. "I'm so sorry. I totally spaced out telling you I was working for Toby today. Since Greg has had him working full-time-plus due to the murder, he couldn't work the Sunday shift. And we're so shorthanded anyway. Deek's been working overtime and Aunt Jackie—well, she's moving in with Harrold. So it was just me." I turned the key in the lock and stepped inside, closing the door before Emma could even look outside. My dog is smart, but when she wants something, she becomes brilliant. And we hadn't run for a few days.

"Oh. So why didn't you pick up? Were you that busy?"

I could tell from her tone she was calming down and not quite as angry, but I knew I'd have to buy brunch next week to get totally out of the doghouse. "No, I had my stupid phone on silent. I just noticed it when I was fumbling around for my keys."

I walked into the kitchen and set the phone on the table, putting it on Speaker. I let Emma out in the backyard and watched for a few minutes.

"Oh, I guess I understand. I was just so excited to show you the linens we have it narrowed down to for the reception."

I must have heard her wrong. "Sorry, I didn't catch that. What did you pick?"

"Nothing yet. I just have it narrowed down to three choices of linens for the tables. They're all white, of course, but each one has a special design I wanted to show you."

I could hear the excitement building in her voice. "So, the venue is providing you choices?"

"No, silly, you have to rent your linen. And your china and flatware. Of course, the venue has basic stuff, but if you want anything suitable, you have to rent." She sighed. "I should have called Jackie. She understands the wedding process so well. She's looking at a fall wedding at that restaurant overlooking the San Francisco Bay. Won't that be lovely? I wish I had that kind of budget, but Justin keeps insisting on keeping it under forty thousand."

"Four thousand? That sounds about right. That doesn't include your dress, right?" I grabbed a water bottle and sat at the table, opening my laptop.

"Forty thousand. You can't even rent a suitable venue for four." She paused as I gulped. "What did you spend on your first wedding?"

"Maybe a thousand, but that included the trip to Vegas. We didn't have a big, expensive event."

"And see how that marriage went?" She paused. "Justin is calling, I need to take this so we can make the final linen decision. I'll call you later."

She hung up before I could say goodbye. Forty thousand. That was ludicrous. And she thought Aunt Jackie was spending more? Unless Harrold was draining his retirement account, I didn't know where they were going to get that kind of money. I put "call Aunt Jackie" on my Monday list.

Putting aside the crazy wedding talk, I focused on the discussion I'd had with Deek about the missing Mrs. Gleason. Then I went into my office and sorted through the ARCs I'd read that month. I needed to take them back to the store, but Toby read only military history and high fantasy. And Deek was focusing on the autobiographies and nonfiction. That meant Aunt Jackie and I shared the rest of the fiction genres. And she hadn't been reading as much as she had before she'd made up with Harrold. I pulled out my three top runners for my favorites and put all the others into large book totes. Then I put the totes into my Jeep. At least that would be done sometime tomorrow, when I ran my errands.

I went back into the kitchen, let in Emma, and thumbed through the books. Settling on one, I sat down to write the recommendation. It had to have the feel of the book without just telling the story. More of a marketing blurb than a true summary. And I always liked to end it with the phrase, "if you liked this, you'll love that."

Two cookies and an hour later, my review was done and I was thinking about another book. I'd brought it home at the beginning of the week and it called to me. I poured a glass of tea and went to the living room to curl up on the couch.

The best thing about the murder mystery I had chosen? No one was getting married or talking about wives or husbands or missing people. I could lose myself in the fantasy without being drawn back into reality. Which was the sign of an excellent book.

Maybe I should use this one for next month's recommendation and end the piece with "Keeps you safe from crazy friends and relatives and out of murder investigations." Because it certainly did that for me.

Chapter 17

I never set alarms for Mondays because I never worked that shift, but this morning, I didn't need one. I glanced at the clock and then threw a pillow over my head. What good was having a day off if you woke up at the same time? I lay that way for a while, then gave up. Greg was cooking bacon downstairs in the kitchen, and I could smell the goodness through the pillow.

By the time I got ready and downstairs, he was sitting at the table eating and talking to Emma. Since he'd moved in, this had been their routine. Breakfast together as long as he didn't have to run off to work. She'd sit by the door and drool at whatever he'd been cooking, and he'd talk to her about his day. It was messed up and totally cute. And I loved both of them more for this interaction.

"There she is. Finally woke up, huh?" He turned his head toward me, and I leaned in for a kiss. "I thought you were going to sleep the day away."

"I don't have to work. I deserve one day to get up past, what is it? Six thirty?" I moved over to the coffeepot and poured myself a cup.

"Almost seven." He glanced at his watch. "I don't have to be in until nine, so I wanted to talk a little before I went in. Your breakfast is in the microwave."

"Uh-oh. What did I do wrong? You never fix me breakfast." I set down the coffee and grabbed the plate of eggs, bacon, and English muffin out of the microwave.

"One, that's not true. And two, you aren't in trouble. I just wanted to talk about Deek's questions. I thought they were well-thought-out and spot-on. Who knew he had it in him?"

"You're always picking on the kid. How come?" I dug into the eggs and ladled a piece onto the muffin before I took a bite.

"He's just so fun to mess with. I know I can't really intimidate him as much as it seems, right?" Greg looked at Emma and pointed to the dog bowl. "Your breakfast is over there. I filled it up this morning." Emma lay down by the door and gave me the sad eyes.

"Anyway, I just wanted you to tell him he did a great job with his analysis. He should think about taking the police entrance exam." He pointed to an article in the newspaper. "Darla's done it again. I don't know why I even investigate; she's always got a perfect suspect rounded up for me."

"But she's always wrong." I took the paper from him. "'*Mike Masters's coincidental arrival in South Cove is being investigated carefully by an unnamed source at South Cove's police department. Will he be able to attend his author signing on Thursday, or will he be too busy with a different type of interview across the street at City Hall?*' I can't believe she gets away with this kind of reporting. Can't he sue her?"

"She didn't say he committed a crime. Only that we are looking at him, which we are. So it's not even untrue." Greg took his plate to the sink. He refilled his coffee. "You've been kind of focused on Alice. What do you think of Mike as a possible murder mastermind?"

"He's good at planning. As an author, he has to be." I thrummed my fingers on the desk. "He's really focused on preserving California history, so it doesn't make sense why he'd kill Frank. They were on the same side."

"Frank's financials look a little suspicious. He got a large deposit every month for the last year of just under ten thousand dollars. Maybe it's from an investment or another account, but it looks suspicious. I've got Toby working with the bank to track down the source."

"What are you saying, that Mike paid Frank money for some reason? And he killed him to be able to stop paying?" I shook my head. "I don't think Mike's books make him the kind of dough that he'd have the funding for that."

"If not Mike, who else would be paying off a certifier of historical sights?" Greg watched my face as awareness flowed into my brain.

I blame the lack of enough coffee, but I finally got it. "You think the developer was paying him off."

"Maybe. If not this developer, another one. And maybe South Cove just got unlucky that the event happened here." He rubbed his hands over his face. "I'm beat and at a loss. We've got some leads to follow, but it seems like we just get one line tied up and six more fall down. Besides, my money's on the ex-wife."

"Which one?" I asked, but I thought I knew the answer. The first Mrs. Gleason, who seemed so reasonable and not at all upset that the man she'd been married to had been run down in the road.

"The first one. The power of a woman scorned times five." He stood and kissed my head. "I'm going to go check the fax machine. Toby's supposed to be sending something over."

"It might need paper," I called after him. My mind was racing with ideas while I finished my breakfast. He still wasn't back when I did, so I rinsed the dishes and put everything in the dishwasher. Except for our coffee cups. I wondered if I should make a pot or just keep using the pod machine. I'd probably drink the entire pot if I made it, minus the cup or two Greg would drink. I decided to take a chance.

The pot had just finished brewing when he came back into the room. "Sorry. Toby called about a stop he'd made last night. He wanted to make sure his paperwork was covered."

"He's done more than a few traffic stops during his tenure. What was so special about this one?" I refilled his cup and placed it on the table next to him. But I had a bad feeling that our morning together had just been canceled.

"I'm going upstairs to get ready. I have to go in." He took the coffee. "Thanks for this. I'll take a thermos too, if you want to make one."

"You made breakfast, I can make a pot of coffee."

He leaned down to kiss me. "You're amazing. And the stop was a DUI."

"He's the DUI king. Didn't you say he's done more than you and Tim combined?" I still wasn't getting why Toby was worried.

"He's never arrested a standing City Council member before. Alice Carroll is sitting in my drunk tank as we speak." He glanced at the clock. "And I've got to get down there before her lawyer shows up and starts browbeating Toby into saying something stupid."

"Alice Carroll? Wow." I sat down at the table and opened my laptop. "Darla's going to have a field day with this."

"Just don't tell anyone you know until it leaks. I just thought you might feel a little satisfaction that the store should be fine because the vandal ringleader was in jail last night."

I shook my head. "She still could have called someone."

"Not from my jail. Toby didn't even let her call her lawyer until this morning, when she sobered up."

"Wait, if Toby's still at the station, who opened the store?" I reached for the phone.

Greg held up a finger. "I knew there was something else. He switched with Deek. He's doing his shift tomorrow."

"I don't know why we even try to have a schedule. They're always changing it." I opened my laptop and looked at my calendar. "Do I need to go to the store for anything?"

Greg shook his head. "I'm good. And dinner will be catch-as-catch-can. I might not be home tonight with this new development."

"And next weekend, we're in Vegas," I reminded him.

He leaned against the edge of the stairway, watching me. "You might have to go alone. Are we driving or flying?"

"Seven-hour drive, three-hour flight for about one hundred dollars each way. I think we should fly." I looked up from the laptop. "But I guess I'd better get tickets if we're flying. I know Aunt Jackie and Harrold are driving up a day early. Which is another shift I have to cover. I really need to hire someone else."

"I'll tell you tomorrow. I know it's short notice, but if I can only get away last minute, I'll either try to get a flight or drive up. Then you can drive back with me and we'll save the return flight for another trip."

"Sounds like a plan." I made a note on tomorrow's calendar. "I hate that you might not be able to go. Aunt Jackie was pretty excited about this Sunday dinner thing."

"At worst, I'll drive up late Saturday and we can still do that. But you might have to drive me back. I'll probably sleep in the car." His phone buzzed with a text. He read it and responded. "I've got to go. She's getting vocal and it's worrying Toby."

She grinned as he ran upstairs. "But I bet you're still going to shower first."

"Of course. I can't go to work smelly. She can wait ten minutes before chewing my butt about Toby's unwillingness to let her go home." He disappeared up the stairs.

"Some people," I said to Emma. She doggy grinned at me like she totally agreed. But she typically agreed with me as long as Greg wasn't there with her favorite treat or offering her a ride in his truck. I got out a piece of paper and started writing my to-do list. I had to go into Bakerstown because Emma was almost out of food. And if Esmeralda was going to check on her, she needed enough to get her through next weekend.

Amy had invited Esmeralda to go, but this was a busy weekend for her other job. She had lots of clients coming in due to the moon's positioning. Which was great for me, because both Toby and Greg were going to Vegas to hang out with Justin. We'd already made plans to shorten hours at the shop to just Deek's shift. I hoped Amy had made her choice and the arrangements like she'd said, or we'd just be hanging out at the casino or walking the strip looking at the sights.

I added "call Sadie" to the list. One, I needed to let her know that we'd be closed, so we didn't need a large order this weekend. And two, I wanted to feel her out about Nick and his summer plans. I sure hoped I could count on him. I glanced at the clock. It was almost eight. If I didn't call now, she'd be down until after noon with her nap.

She picked up on the first ring. "I know why you're calling. I'll come by on Friday morning and refill what you need. Lille's did a double order of desserts, knowing you'd be closed up most of the day."

"Well, I'm glad everyone is excited about me being out of town this weekend." I kept writing notes on my to-do list as we talked.

"She's just expecting more traffic, that's all." Sadie always saw the good side of things. "Bill is taking me out to dinner after services on Sunday. He's such a kind man."

Oh, it was Bill now, not Pastor Bill. I was happy for my friend. She deserved a good man in her life. "That will be fun. Hey, have you heard from Nick lately? Did you ask him what his summer plans are?"

A pause over the line told me my answer before she responded. "He's got an amazing opportunity in London this year. He's working for a law firm in their administration department."

"What? He'd rather do that than sell coffee out of a hot food truck at festivals?" I joked. "That sounds awesome. Is he coming home first?"

"No. He's going straight from school. I guess he's all grown-up now."

I heard the wistfulness in my friend's voice. Nick's change in plans had hurt her. "You'll always be his mom."

"It's silly, I know. I was just so excited to do our summer stuff. Like the first beach visit of the season. And a trip to the Castle for a swim. We always went into the city for a week's vacation." She paused. "But this is an amazing opportunity for his future. I can't be selfish."

"Maybe he'll come home before he goes back to school."

Sadie's voice brightened. "He is. He'll be here a week before he goes back. I guess next year will be the same. I'll just have to make my own summer plans, right?"

"Exactly. Maybe there's someone nearby who'd like to do those things?"

She chuckled. "Stop teasing me about Bill. We're taking this slow. He's got a lot on his plate right now."

"You better be a big part of that plate," I chided. "You deserve to be treated like a queen."

"You're a good friend. You know just what to say to get me out of the dumps."

I crossed Nick off my list. "I was the one who put you there, so I should be willing to help. I'll see you tomorrow at the shop."

"Bright and early."

We said our goodbyes and I hung up. I went through my computer files and found the last ad we'd run to get staff. I pasted it into an email to my aunt and asked if I should post this in the newspaper and maybe in our newsletter. I heard the responding *bing* just a few minutes after I'd pushed send. "That was quick," I said to the empty kitchen.

My aunt had sent me a one-line response. "I think I have someone."

I emailed back a question: "Who?"

No answer this time. I went and cleaned both bathrooms and scratched that off the list. Then I checked my email again. Still no answer from Aunt Jackie, but one from Deek.

The gist of the email was about the signing on Thursday. He'd tried to get Masters to wait so he could gather more buzz, but apparently, the guy was planning on leaving next week. I wondered if Greg knew that. I responded back that it wasn't a problem. We'd had a sign up for a few days, and Deek had posted it on our web page as soon as it was scheduled. If Mike didn't get the turnout he wanted, it wasn't because of our lack of trying. We were selling his books with a commission fee, so I didn't even have to order books. I'd emailed Sadie to leave a couple dozen cookies for us tomorrow, but other than that, the signing was in the book god's hands.

I added a note to my talk with my aunt about the new hire for tomorrow's list. Then I finished the tasks in my email and took a quick peek at flight schedules for the weekend. We could still get on a late Friday or early Saturday flight, but anything after noon and I'd be pushing the party time too close. Greg just might miss his time with the boys. But even murder wouldn't be a good enough excuse for me to miss out on Amy's bachelorette party.

Even if it was my own demise.

Chapter 18

When I got to Bakerstown, instead of going straight to the pet store for Emma's food, I made a quick stop at the Bakerstown Funeral Home. Doc Ames probably couldn't give me any more insight into Frank's death than I already had, especially because I'd witnessed the event, but I hadn't seen him for a while. I took out the box of cookies I'd stopped to get at the shop when I parked and made my way inside the large doors into the chilly, formal waiting area. It gave me the chills every time I came inside. I guess I wasn't as comfortable with the thought of death as my investigation habit would suggest. The velvet curtains and deep, dark carpet always reminded me of a gothic horror flick. I expected someone with a vampire cape and blood dripping from their lips to come out of one of the chapel doors at any time.

When Doc popped out of the chapel, I barely concealed the little squeak that came out of my mouth.

He grinned because he'd actually heard it or saw it on my face. "Sorry to startle you. But aren't you a sight for sore eyes today? I was just thinking I hadn't seen you around for a while. How's South Cove?"

"Crazy as ever." I followed him into his office and was relieved to be in the crowded room with stacks of papers cluttering his desk and the credenza behind it. He poured two cups of coffee and I opened the box of cookies, laying Coffee, Books, and More napkins next to the box. I told him about Bill's father and his absence, along with the attacks on the shop since Alice had put out the increase in Business-2-Business fees. "She even changed the name to add that cute little two numeral in the middle, instead of a real word. Amy overheard her talking about moving the meetings to Lille's."

"I'm not sure Lille would enjoy the attention of the Council once a month. She loves customers, but hates the one-on-one with people. That's why Carrie is her most important asset. She uses that woman way past her job duties as a waitress."

Interesting. I hadn't even known that Doc Ames knew Carrie. Was there a bit of a crush here? Greg said I was always looking for a matchmaking opportunity. I decided to think on that one a little more. "Yeah, that's what I was thinking."

We sat and ate the cookies in comfortable silence. Finally, he brushed crumbs off his hands. "I suspect you're here about Frank?"

"Actually, no. I just wanted to stop in. It's been a while since we visited." I sipped my coffee. I wanted a third cookie, but I restrained myself. I'd planned on stopping at the ice cream shop on the way home from Bakerstown. Living in sunny California made ice cream a year-round necessity. At least in my mind.

"Oh, well, then I guess I won't tell you that he was being slowly poisoned. If the damage from the truck hadn't killed him, Frank would have been dead in a week or two, tops. At least if he'd kept getting his daily dose of poison."

"Shut the front door." I stared at him. "Seriously? I thought this was an open-and-shut case of hit-and-run."

"So did I when the body first came into the building. I always do toxicology screens, just in case, but I'd noticed an odd tinge to his fingernails. I thought it might just be road dust because your main street is all brick, but I added a few additional tests. Did I hit pay dirt or what? Greg certainly was surprised when I called. But he did say I probably ruined his weekend. Did you two have plans?"

I told him all about Amy's party trip to Vegas after we got off work on Friday. "But now, I guess Greg's going to be driving to Vegas alone on Saturday night. I should just tell my aunt we can't make dinner on Sunday."

He shook his head. "No, I think you and Greg should definitely go to Vegas and to this dinner. It's not often you get to spend time with friends and family. In my job, you see a lot of people with a lot of regrets. Don't let this weekend be one of yours."

"Wow, way to put choices in perspective. It's just a dinner." I held up my hand to ward off the response that I saw forming on his face. "But you're right. My aunt and Harrold are older and none of us are promised tomorrow, so we'll go. I just don't like him driving alone."

"Why don't you wait for him?"

I finished my coffee. "I would, but then I'd miss Amy's thing. And right now, as crazy as she is about this wedding, I don't know if she'd ever forgive me if I missed her party."

"Never get in between a woman and her wedding fantasy." The phone started ringing. "I'm sorry, I should get that."

"No worries. I need to run and get Emma some food anyway. See you soon. And thanks for the great gossip." I waved and backed out of the room, trying not to eavesdrop on the phone conversation. As the county coroner, Doc Ames had access to all sorts of interesting things. Most of which Greg wanted me to stay out of. I knew he probably shouldn't tell me half the things he did, but he also knew I wasn't going to go blabbing what I'd heard all over town. No matter what Darla did to me.

I headed to the pet supply store, and thought about who in Frank's life would have benefited from his death. I wondered if Greg had talked to the lawyer about the will yet. Did the trail of murder run side by side with the trail of money?

I couldn't think of what reason I could give an attorney to get additional information about Frank. I could lie and say I worked with Greg. And I did, technically. We worked last month on the back gardens up against the house. They were beautiful now and the lilies were just starting to fan out and fill the planter boxes.

But that was probably pushing the definition. Especially if Greg found out. I consoled myself with a milkshake on the way home. And I'd gotten Emma a new stuffed animal I would give her before I left for the weekend. I hated for my dog to be sad. It was bad enough that Toby wasn't going to be able to watch her this weekend. But she liked Esmeralda too. Emma probably held a doggy party on the back deck when we were out of town.

Or maybe not.

When I got home, I decided to let the rest of the to-do list set for the next time I did housecleaning. Which would be two weeks if we stayed in Vegas as long as we were planning. Or, if I drove back with Greg, it would be next week, when I drove him home.

I picked up a new book and fell into the story. Greg found me there close to six and showed mercy on me. He'd brought home a Diamond Lille's fried chicken box.

Life was good.

* * * *

Good, but busy. I spent all day on Tuesday, Wednesday, and Thursday getting ready to be away on the weekend. We had books to order, payroll to finalize, and, of course, it was the end of the month, so the accountant wanted our books and receipts on Friday. Aunt Jackie had been too busy moving to do any of the monthly reports. I shouldn't gripe about doing them, except she hadn't warned me. I'd assumed she was handling them, but apparently, she and Harrold were spending her shift talking and mooning over each other and making plans for a honeymoon that was over a year away. Who does that?

By the end of my shift on Thursday, I was ready to sell the store, marry Greg, and become a stay-at-home mom with twelve kids. I just didn't know if he would rubber-stamp the plan.

I stopped at Diamond Lille's for lunch on my way home. I was still driving back and forth to work, which seemed totally stupid, but it made Greg feel better. In the morning, Emma whined and stared at her leash, but we were banned from the beach as well. I'd just ordered food and had my iced tea and a book open when my phone rang.

"I'm not coming back," I said to Toby. I knew his cell number. And my phone showed a picture of whoever was calling. As long as I'd set it up right.

He chuckled. "I'm not calling you back. Greg called looking for you. He said you could go running today if you wanted."

I sat up straighter. "He caught the guy?"

"No such luck. But they found the truck. Parked in the art district in the city. Apparently, it had a few parking tickets, so when the cop who was going to tow it ran the plates, he found our APB."

"They just dumped it?"

"It looks that way. Anyway, Greg said you need to run before you and Emma go off the deep end. But be careful. Just because the truck's in police custody getting dusted and gone over for evidence doesn't mean we're even close to finding the killer."

That was true. "Hey, I heard you cornered a famous DUI this weekend."

"Famous in her own mind. Man, Alice was hot when I pulled her over. I've never heard a woman swear so much. In fact, I've never heard anyone swear that much. She told me she'd have my badge by Monday noon."

"How'd that work out for her?" I asked as Carrie set a plate with a Cuban sandwich and wedge fries in front of me. I might have started drooling.

"She stomped out of the station with her lawyer Monday morning and I haven't heard a word. Greg talked to Mayor Baylor for about five minutes, but I'm still a deputy."

"Who did his job." I picked up a waffle fry. "My food is here, so I'm hanging up. I'll be home in a few and I'll text you when I leave to run and when we're back. How does that work?"

"Sounds like a plan. I've got to go. The cosmetology school group just arrived. I guess they heard I'm working today."

As I hung up the phone, I thought it probably didn't matter if it was Toby or Deek, the women would have come. I just didn't want to say that aloud to Toby. He could keep his delusion.

After getting the good news that I was no longer on house arrest, I ate quickly and got ready to go home and get my dog. Carrie came by with my bill, and I studied her as she refilled my glass of tea. "I didn't know you knew Doc Ames."

She eyed me suspiciously. "How do you know who I know?"

"Doc mentioned you. He said you were Lille's public face with customers." I pulled out my credit card and put it on the check without looking at the bill. "He seemed to know a lot about you. Are you friends?"

"Yeah, we're friends. He's a nice man." Carrie picked up the check and the card, her face beet red. "I'll get this right back to you."

I watched her almost sprint back to the cash register, where she ran my card, then handed the receipt and a pen to another waitress. Then Carrie disappeared into the back. I'd hit the nail on the head. They were either in a relationship or thinking about one. I guess love was in the air in South Cove this spring.

At home, I got Emma ready and we went down to the beach to run. I'd slowed down on scarfing all my lunch, so I thought I'd be okay, but I decided to take the first little bit slower than normal. Emma was enjoying playing in the surf. And there wasn't another soul on the beach, so I let her off the leash.

Just as she went running to play in the waves, I realized my mistake. There was someone else on the beach; they were just away ahead of us. It appeared to be a man, larger than average, and dressed in jeans and a plain tee. And he was walking straight for me. I was glad I'd reached out to Toby when I left. If I was going to be kidnapped or killed in the next few minutes, someone would find Emma sooner rather than later. I'd hate to have her get hit on the road, trying to get home. She's not the best at watching for cars.

I pushed my negative thoughts away. Just because I was alone on a beach with a man didn't mean anything bad was going to happen. Greg had me jumpy after the house arrest the last few days. I called Emma to me and clicked back on the leash. She sat at my feet, not happy about the change in plans, but not whining either. I guess she was just glad to be out of the house too. We started walking down the beach in the direction of the other person.

I hadn't gone too far before I recognized him. And I didn't know if I would rather have an unknown person or have to talk with Mike Masters again. I'd told Toby and Aunt Jackie that I was too busy to attend the writer event that evening. Now he was going to see me out relaxing on the beach with my dog. I thought up a quick lie in case he asked. I had to go into town for a wake for a friend. No one would push on that excuse.

He raised a hand as we got closer. "I'm so glad I ran into you. I felt bad not asking you specifically about the signing tonight, but that guy you have working there, he's so good at the marketing part. The local paper came to interview me early this week and the interview was in the paper this morning. I hope we get a lot of visitors."

"Me too. I'm glad you scheduled an event. Deek said you were leaving town soon?"

He nodded, scanning the ocean waves as he spoke. "Yeah, my mom's not doing well and I need to get back to Henderson to check on her. But I'm going to miss this place. A lot. I wish I could afford to live here."

"I think California's pricey everywhere, but on the beach listings have to be worse." I felt lucky that Miss Emily had left me the house. If not, I'd still be living in the small apartment over the store. So much had happened during the last few years. My aunt had moved in and moved out. And now the apartment would have a new person enjoying its homey comfort. I stopped myself from mentioning I might have a rental available mostly because my aunt had said she had someone. It wasn't just because I didn't really like Mike. At least, that was what I was going to tell myself.

"I haven't even looked. I support myself with my writing, but not at beach-house level." He smiled and leaned down to pet Emma. "Who's a good dog?"

Emma greeted him like they were old friends. She barked out a greeting, then sat to let him rub behind her ears. My dog likes everyone.

"Well, we'd better get going. I'm on a tight schedule today."

He looked up at me. "Are you going to be able to come to the signing? I'd love to see you there. It's good for the readers to know that the owner supports author events."

Great, now I was getting the guilt lecture. I shook my head and moved around him. "Sorry, I've got an appointment tonight. Too bad the signing was so rushed. I would have loved to be there."

I didn't want Mike to see my nose grow, so I started running. I called back, "Have a great signing."

We got a few feet away when I heard his answer. "Thanks for everything."
Wow, did I feel like a heel. But he had started it with the guilt comment.
Yet somehow, I knew karma was going to slap me hard about this encounter.
I just hoped it wouldn't be too soon. Emma barked, and when I looked
down, she was doggy grinning at me. "You're happy to be out here
again, aren't you?"

She bounced in her gait, then barked again, clearly pleased with
her situation.

Her happiness made my heart swell. I might not be able to make everyone
happy, but I did a good job with Emma. And, most of the time, with Greg.
And even myself, at times. And that's all I could be responsible for. The
rest of the world was on its own.

When I got back home, I texted Toby and then sat at the table going
through my mail. A letter from the Heritage Society fell out between the
light bill and the water bill. Crap. I knew I'd forgotten to do something
on Monday. I'd been planning on going to talk to them to see what they
knew about what Frank was working on.

I opened the letter. It was in response to my voice mail. Skimming the
letter, they said they couldn't move the wall back on the list to be explored
without a new application. I frowned and read a line aloud. "'When you
removed the wall from consideration, you stopped all forward movement
of the process.' Wait, what? I didn't remove it."

I dialed the number at the top of the letter, and a perky voice answered the
phone. "California Heritage Society. This is Paxton, how can I help you?"

I explained who I was and that I'd gotten a letter saying to reapply.

"Yes, ma'am. I have your file pulled up here. Because the investigation
has been closed, we need a new application. That way we have the most
current information on you."

She seemed so reasonable. "Okay, but I'm confused. The letter said that
I closed the case. And I didn't. The last I knew, it was still on the docket."

"Okay, well, the computer shows it's closed. Hold on, let me review the
notes." A humming sound filled my ears, and I realized Paxton had put
me on hold and I was listening to a washed-out version of "Tie a Yellow
Ribbon." I took advantage of the time and went to the fridge for a bottle
of water. I refilled Emma's bowl as well.

When Paxton returned, she sounded less perky. "Are you sure you
didn't close the file? The note here says you called in last month and said
you were tired of waiting and were going to sell the property."

"One, I don't think I'll ever sell the house, so if that's what it said, I
didn't call. Don't you need a verified letter or something to close a file?"

"Yes, we would have sent out a letter and then closed it after we got it back." She paused, and I could hear keys clacking. She was looking for the letter. "But there's nothing in the file. Look, I can't change the file, but I'm taking this to my manager. Can I get your phone number and call you back when we decide what we can do on this?"

I decided I didn't have time to do any more fighting, so I agreed. At least it was a step in the right direction. "When should I hear from you about the reopening?"

"Next week at the latest. She's already gone for the day, and I know she's going to want to talk to everyone, but we may be able to reopen it because it looks like it was an error."

After I'd hung up, I wondered if it had been an actual error, or if this was one more of the dirty tricks Alice had been playing. Once this weekend was over, that woman and I were going to have a long heart-to-heart. And she wasn't going to like what I had to say.

Chapter 19

Friday morning, after the commuters arrived and left just as quickly, the shop was slow. Probably not any slower than normal, but I was getting on a plane in a few hours. Without Greg. I glanced at the clock for the hundredth time and only five minutes had passed. I really loved traveling, but I'm one of those who, once I decided to do something, I wanted it done now.

I was working until two so Deek could have the morning to write before working both his shortened shift and Aunt Jackie's. She and Harrold had probably already left town as they were driving. We had rooms in Treasure Island, mostly because I liked the irony. Amy had been stranded on an island for over a week a few years ago and she didn't even realize there was a problem. The girl could live and enjoy herself anywhere.

I eyed the dessert display again. I'd already eaten breakfast, but come two, it was vacation time. And vacation meant I could eat whatever I wanted with no regrets.

The bell rang over the door, and my aunt waltzed into the store with Harrold at her side. She had on white capris and a pink flowered shirt, along with sandals. I guessed she'd gotten the vacation memo too. "Good, you're here."

"Where else would I be? It's my shift." Okay, so that sounded a little grumpy. "What's going on? I thought you would be on the road by now."

"And we would have, but your aunt insisted on checking in on you. I told her everything would be fine, but you know Jackie." Harrold stepped close and gave me a kiss on the cheek. "How are you? Are you looking forward to visiting Sin City?"

"I have my quarters for the slots right here." I pointed to my bag. Okay, so I didn't really have quarters, but I had an envelope filled with gambling money. Once it was gone, I was done. But I wanted to play a little blackjack while we were there. "What about you?"

"Dear, I am the king of the penny slots. I will come out of our weekend richer than I went in. That I promise you." He winked at my aunt.

"You always do." Aunt Jackie touched his arm. "Anyway, I told Mr. Masters he could pick up his check this morning for the books we sold. I put an envelope in the cash drawer. Make sure he signs the receipt I have on the front and put that back into the drawer."

"We usually mail their commission checks." I opened the drawer and saw the envelope. Almost three hundred dollars. He hadn't done bad for short notice. "He must have gotten quite the audience."

"He did, surprisingly. And he has a good talk. People liked him." My aunt looked like she'd swallowed something bad. "Deek did good by signing him up. We should have him come back next year."

"Now was that so hard to say?" I smiled at my aunt. "I'm flying up, so I'll probably beat you there, but Greg won't be in until sometime Saturday night."

"That too bad that he'll miss the men's night. We have some debauchery planned." Harrold grinned. "Wild women, booze, and cards. What's not to love?"

"As long as he's there on Sunday, we're fine." My aunt peered at me. "He will be there, right?"

"He says he will. But you know his job might keep him here if things blow up." I didn't get Aunt Jackie. One minute she was harping on me to understand Greg's work schedule, and now she was pushing to make sure he was at a dinner. She must have nabbed some fancy chef for this. "I promise he'll do his best."

"I'm sure he will." Harrold put an arm around my aunt and the two of them exchanged a glance.

I saw my aunt's shoulders drop in surrender. Man, Harrold was like a lion tamer with my aunt. He knew just what buttons to push. A tactic I'd never figured out. Which was why we were usually on each other's last nerve.

"Well, then, we'll just have to think good thoughts." My aunt smiled up at Harrold. Then turned toward me. "I left Deek an open-and-close list because he'll only have a short day tomorrow. And I have a more extensive list for tonight. He does know how to make a bank drop, correct?"

"Yes, he's done it before." Of course she knew this, but my aunt was a bit of a control freak hanging out under that designer cruise wear. "The shop will be fine, but we really need to hire someone now. Nick's not coming home this summer; we've probably lost him to adulthood."

"Children do grow up." She glanced at her watch. "We'll talk about the new hire on Tuesday morning. I've invited her to the staff meeting. We really need to go."

I stood with my mouth open as I watched her and Harrold start to leave the room. "Wait. You hired someone. Just like that?"

"She has excellent references. I know you're going to love her." Aunt Jackie didn't even turn around. They just continued out the door.

I couldn't believe she had just hired someone without talking to me. Well, I guess I could. She'd done it before. She'd hired Toby without me even knowing we needed another person. And before I knew she was staying on as a manager. She'd supposed to be here just covering the store and before the month was out, she was moved into the apartment and telling me what to do with my life and my shop. Family. You had to accept them as they were because you weren't going to change them.

Even if they had a supercool boyfriend like Harrold.

I went back to the chores list she'd left Deek. I was too worked up to just sit and read, so I'd get a few of these marked off before he even arrived. As it worked out, Deek only had three things left on the list when he came into work: clean the coffeepots, restock the display case, and make the bank deposit.

I'd been busy. I glanced around the shining dining room and the fully stocked bookshelves and felt a sense of completion. I liked working my shop. I loved stocking new books, smelling the fresh paper book smell as I did. And finding gems that I'd thought about reading that had fallen off my radar. I had three in my tote for the weekend. I should make a good dent in the pile before I got back into town on Monday.

Several customers were scattered around the store. Mostly in small groups, talking and sipping coffee. But one sat alone. It was a woman I'd talked to earlier, but I didn't think I remembered her name. I'd have to make sure to look at her credit card the next time she visited. She was quickly becoming a regular. Today, her braids were wound around her head and she looked more like a librarian than the heading-to-the-beach look I'd seen her wear the first time I'd met her.

"Hey, boss, the place looks great. I take it you must be out of reading material." Deek stuffed his bicycle bag in the back room and then came back out to wash his hands and put on the Coffee, Books, and More aprons we had all our baristas wear. Which reminded me, we needed a new order, and I wanted a new logo or saying for the front before we did.

"Ha, ha. I just get nervous before I travel." I slipped off my apron but spread it out on the counter. "Do you think you could design a few ideas for a new order? I'd like to do something fun, either book- or coffee-focused."

"Sure, if you don't mind. I've got some ideas already." He grinned, looking pleased to be asked.

"I figured. You're so good at the marketing side of the business. If I had a bigger budget, I'd hire you to just do that. As it is, we need baristas more." I picked up my travel purse. I'd stuffed the new books inside the tote, but I'd put at least one in my carry-on before I got to the airport.

"Even after Jackie's new hire?"

Deek's question shocked me. Not only had my aunt *not* mentioned this to me, she'd already told Deek? "You knew?"

He shrugged his shoulders and avoided my eyes. "Look, I don't want to cause an issue. I'm just easy to talk to."

"Well, my aunt is going to have some quality time talking to me in the near future." I refilled my coffee mug. "You have my cell and Jackie's in case something goes wrong. Greg will be here at least until late Saturday, but Toby's leaving early Saturday morning, as soon as he gets off shift. So you really are on your own. If something happens, just close the shop. We can make up the revenue some other time."

"Heck no. I'm King of the World now, with everyone gone. I'm going to rearrange all the bookshelves and order a ton of treats. You'll be amazed and overwhelmed when you get back." He leaned his head on his hands, watching me.

"As long as you stay within budget, I don't care." I moved to the back door. "Seriously if something happens, call me."

"Nothing is going to happen." He met my gaze. He knew what I was worried about, and he was telling me to trust him. "Deek is on the job."

I laughed, letting the unease settle. "Anyway, call me if you need anything."

"You always have to put a damper on my take-over-the-world plans," he called after me.

"Even the CEO of Starbucks has a budget," I called back. "Don't have too much fun."

As I made my way into the California sunshine, I was smiling. We might be a minicrew right now, but the people who worked for me were family. Not just people who wanted jobs. They cared almost as much as I did about the shop and customer service. I had the best job ever. Of course, I was a small business owner. It wasn't really a job; it was a lifestyle. One that gave me the ultimate access to my two favorite things: coffee and books.

I waved to Emma as I drove past the house. She couldn't see me, of course, because she was probably sleeping inside in the kitchen. I'd dropped by Esmeralda's last night to give her my schedule and hotel information and let her know where the treats were stored. Her cat, Maggie, had immediately jumped up into my arms and given me kitty hugs. What can I say? Animals love me.

Esmeralda had a client at her fortune-telling shop, judging by the Rolls-Royce in her driveway. I didn't know why she even stayed working as the part-time police dispatcher; her side business had to be raking in the moola. I didn't understand what she really did. She called it "reading people with a little extra." She had told me before that I had a touch of the gift, but if it was anything like I'd experienced with Masters and the kidnapping vision, I'd rather return the gift unopened.

As I drove to the airport, I thought about that experience and whether it meant anything to the murder investigation Greg was trying to solve. I didn't see how. Frank had been hit right in front of me. No one had put a cloth with sleeping gas or whatever over his face. Maybe the simplest answer was the easiest. I had been too tired and had slipped into a waking dream. I'd heard of things like that happening to people.

Satisfied I'd found an answer that didn't involve me being crazy or psychic, I pulled into the long-term parking lot and went inside to go through security and find my gate. Once I competed that, I found a coffee shop and ordered a large coffee and a bottle of water for the plane. Then I settled into one of the less-than-comfortable chairs and pulled out a book. I let out a little sigh of pleasure as I cracked the spine.

Out of the corner of my eye, I saw a familiar face. I was facing the entrance where the TSA-precheck passengers came through security. A man in a black suit glanced my way, then turned to go in the opposite direction. If I didn't know better, I would have sworn it was Mike Masters. He hadn't come into the shop to pick up his check, and there was no way he could have already done that and beat me to the airport. Besides, Mike wore jeans and T-shirts. Or had every time I'd seen him. Formal business attire was not his jam.

I seriously needed some time away from South Cove and Frank's murder. I was beginning to see things. Okay, so I'd been doing that for a while, but this just confirmed that I needed a weekend filled with fun, laughter, good food, and several adult beverages. And I wasn't thinking of coffee.

I returned to the book and started reading. Chapter one.

* * * *

By the time I landed at McCarran International Airport in Vegas, I'd almost finished the first book. It was a woman's fiction summer read and put me in the mood for a frozen drink by the pool. The slots at the airport were filled with travelers on a layover, and everyone seemed to be in a fun-loving mood. I texted Amy as soon as I landed and told her I'd be at the hotel and checked in by five.

She texted back that they'd meet me in the lobby at five thirty for dinner. Which was perfect. I got a taxi and relaxed for the drive into the Strip. The traffic was brutal, but my cab driver kept pointing out all the new attractions. "You should have been here back in the day. I've lived here all my life and all I've seen is change. My wife and I like to go to Fremont Street for date night and try to remember what it was like in the golden days."

I loved the different feel of each of the fantasy hotels. The Venetian tried to take you to Italy. The Paris Casino had the Eiffel Tower. And there was even a hotel shaped like a pyramid. You could go anywhere in the world just by crossing the street. Treasure Island was built for the-pirate loving crowd. Tourists could watch a staged pirate takeover of another boat right outside the casino. Night after night. And I'd heard their buffet was out of this world.

I kicked off my shoes and sprawled on my king-sized bed. I know the flight wasn't that long, but it still sapped my energy. I still had a half hour before I had to meet Amy. I glanced at the book. That should be just enough time for me to read the last few chapters, if I didn't shower and change for dinner.

I compromised and took out a sundress with cute flip-flops. Then I curled up on the bed and finished the book. I could run through the shower, dress, and freshen my makeup in less than ten minutes. I just had to finish reading with that amount of time left.

I missed my goal by three minutes. But I was still in the lobby, dressed, and looking amazing by the time Amy arrived. My friend was typically early, so I counted my blessings. And I had one book read and off my TBR list. It had been a productive day.

"Your aunt and Harrold are having dinner in their room. She just texted me. Darla and Matt aren't here yet; they're driving. So it's just the three of us." She smiled up at Justin. "I've told him tomorrow he can't even call me, so he needs his Amy fix tonight."

"I can grab a bite on my own if you two want to spend some time alone." I thought about the next book waiting for me to crack open the spine. And I really wanted to check out the pool.

"No way you're leaving me alone with her." Justin grabbed my arm and moved in between the two of us. "And we're talking about anything *but* the wedding. No planning. No linens. And for goodness' sake, I'm not eating cake samples for dessert. This weekend is all about fun. Do you think Greg will be here for the guys' night tomorrow?"

We started walking toward the restaurant in the building. "I'm not sure. He's trying, but he wouldn't even let me set up a flight reservation. He's going to either fly up tonight or tomorrow morning or drive up on Saturday if he can't get a flight."

"Well, I hope he can get here. My brother, who's going to be the best man, can't take off this weekend. He just called and he has a big gig on Saturday in Florida. Life of a musician." Justin paused at the host near the entrance. "I hope you like steak."

The place was all old, dark wood and darker colors. Not the type of place I regularly ate, but this wasn't my celebration weekend. "Sounds great," I lied. As we were walking in the dining room with white tablecloths and wineglasses already set on the table, I froze.

There, in a booth, in the black suit I'd seen at the airport, was Mike Masters. He was having dinner with a blond woman who looked suspiciously like the Realtor who'd tried to strong-arm me into selling my house. Our host set us at a table and I excused myself. "I think I know that couple. I'll be right back."

Chapter 20

I crossed the room and stood in front of the booth until they both looked up at me. SaraBeth dropped her spoon and Mike threw his napkin on the table.

"Interesting. Your sick mother looks like she's doing better."

"Look, Jill, I can explain." Mike glanced at the woman. "This is Sara Marston. She's my partner."

"You're both in real estate? I don't understand. One of you was trying to get me to sell and one of you was trying to stop me. What was the game? Confusion?" I glanced over at our table, where Amy and Justin were watching me. I nodded that I was fine and turned back to the booth.

"We're not in real estate." He pulled out a card and handed it to me. "As well as being an author, I have a day job. I'm with the FBI. We're investigating Aaron Presley, the developer of the water park."

"I don't understand. Why are you investigating him?" I held up the card to Sara. "I take it you have one of these too?"

She nodded. "Sorry to push you so hard, but I had to know if he'd already gotten to you. I mean, you were under some pretty hard intimidation to sell."

"The attacks on my shop? That was you guys?" Now I was starting to get angry. Why would they do that to me?

Mike held up a hand. "No. That wasn't us. I believe that was Presley and someone from South Cove who was working with him. He really needs your property to get the development funding and grants he wants. Then, once the money is locked up, he'll start by demolishing your house. After that, he'll start having planning and zoning issues, or other delays will happen, and he'll just disappear. I told you before, he's not a nice guy."

"And I told you before, I'm not selling. Look, go use someone else and stop playing with South Cove. If he has to have my house for the project, he's run up against a brick wall anyway. I'm not selling."

"They aren't just going to take your no and go away. The intimidation will get harder."

"I live with a cop."

"That might not be enough." Mike moved over in the booth. "Look, sit down with us and we'll explain our plan. Once we get him cornered, you'll be fine."

"Sorry, I'm with friends." I glanced back at the table, and now Justin was standing up. I shook my head and he sat down. "Call me on Monday and I'll schedule a meeting with you two and Greg. I need his input on this."

"We may not have until Monday," Sara said flatly.

A chill went over my entire body. Maybe I should call Esmeralda and have her move Emma. With Greg and Toby out of town, it might be easy to do something to my house, like set it on fire. The only thing in the house that I couldn't replace was my dog. "You think they'll destroy the house? My dog's in there. You need to put someone there to watch it."

"Like we have the funding for that." She snorted and returned to her steak dinner.

"But you have funding to eat in a place like this." Now I was furious.

"Jill, call me tomorrow and we'll set up a meeting. I don't think you have anything to worry about right now." He glared at his partner. "Sara can be a bit premature."

I pointed at him. "If anything happens to Emma, you're going to be sorry." I walked back to the table, fear chasing me with every step.

Amy put her hand on my shoulder as I dug for my phone. "What's wrong?"

"I'm just a little worried. Let me call Esmeralda and have her go get Emma out of the house. Then I can eat." I glanced at Justin. "Can you order for me? And get me a beer."

I hoped the alcohol would keep my hands from shaking. When the call went through, Esmeralda picked up on the first ring.

"I don't know how you knew, but she's over here with me," Esmeralda said before I could even ask her to get Emma.

"What happened?"

"Someone tried to break into your house. I saw Toby's truck take off about four. I knew you were gone and Greg was still at the office because he'd just called about a file he couldn't find. When the van pulled into the house, I called Greg back, and they caught the guys before they could even pick the lock."

I took a deep breath, tears filling my eyes. "And Emma's okay?"

"She is now. I guess Greg said he could hear her barking when he pulled up behind the van. She was so loud, the guys didn't even hear him come up behind them." Esmerelda laughed. "Right now, she's lying on her bed in my kitchen with Maggie cuddled up next to her. I'm pretty sure she's asleep. She was worn out."

"Thank you. She'll be okay there, right? You don't have any clients coming in who this might be an issue for?"

"Nope. I'm done for the day. I'd rescheduled some of my appointments so I'd have a short day today. I guess a little bird told me I needed to free up some time."

"We'll go with that. Thanks for taking care of her." I was about to hang up when I heard her call my name.

"Jill, when I told him I was calling you, Greg said to tell you that he was on his way as soon as he got these guys set up in a cell for the weekend."

"Thanks. I'll give him a call after dinner." I hung up the phone, and instead of tucking it away, I put it on the table.

"What in the world is going on?" Amy looked at me, then the phone. "Don't tell me something happened to the house."

"No. At least, it didn't because Greg stopped the bad guys." I went on to tell them all about what happened, stopping the story to order food because they'd waited for me to get off the phone. They had ordered drinks, and as soon as my beer arrived, I ignored the chilled glass and drank down half of the bottle. When I ordered my dinner, I added in another beer. "So, long story short, Emma's fine and Greg's on his way here as soon as he gets done locking up the ones who tried to get into the house."

"Do you know what they were looking for?" Justin asked as the waiter started setting food on the table in front of us.

"My guess? After hearing what Mike had to say, I think they were going to set it on fire. And probably steal some easy-to-fence things. We don't have much. But I bet Greg's new television wouldn't have been found in the fire. Or any of the computer stuff in the office." I took another sip of my beer. "I'm just glad Emma's okay."

Amy pointed her fork at Sara and Mike, who were now watching us. Mike was on his phone, apparently getting the same news I'd just received. "What about those two?"

"They're feds. Along with having cover jobs like being an author and a Realtor. She's the one who tried to push me into selling the house." I cut off a piece of my salmon and took a bite. It was heaven. I closed my eyes and enjoyed the taste and sent a prayer of thanks up for Emma's safety. I'd never had to worry about her before. Well, just once when Toby left some chocolate down and she ate it. But that had been an accident, because he'd been fighting with his then-girlfriend, Sasha.

We sat quietly for a while and just ate.

"I'm sorry I pulled you here for a party." Amy put down her fork and took a sip of her margarita. "I knew things were going on. We could have postponed this."

"No."

The emphasis of the word made both Amy and Justin look at me. I'm pretty sure they thought I'd gone a little crazy. I set down my fork and took both their hands. "We have to learn to celebrate the good things in life. Like your upcoming wedding. This party was long overdue. Your engagement party was overshadowed by Aunt Jackie dumping Harrold. You both deserve something that's just for you. And I'm looking forward to celebrating with you."

"That was really sweet of you." Amy leaned over and kissed my cheek. "Thank you."

Justin lifted his drink glass. "To Jill and our South Cove friends. Thank you for making life interesting."

I clinked with the couple, then took a sip. "I'm thinking our lives will never be boring."

"You know, you and Greg could tie the knot this weekend. Just have a Vegas wedding. We'll all be here anyway." Amy took another sip of her margarita, then quickly set it down and reached up to her forehead. "Brain freeze."

Laughing, I went back to my dinner. "Serves you right. What part of this-is-your-weekend didn't you hear?"

I wasn't going to tell her that the thought of being married again scared me. I mean, I loved Greg. That was certain, and we seemed to be well suited for each other. We liked being together and we had a lot to talk about. But what if that died? Where would we be? And what about kids? Did saying yes mean getting a brood of kids started? I worried about leaving my dog for a weekend. What would I do if I had a baby? Who would I trust enough to watch her while we traveled?

My mind was racing and I didn't like any of the questions or answers.

Amy shook my arm. "Earth to Jill. Do you want to go to a show with us? We're going to the circus one. We can get you a ticket."

I finished my second beer. "I think I'm going to go find the pool and sit and read until it's too dark to be outside. Then I'll go to my room and read."

"We came to Vegas for fun." Amy pouted.

I nodded. "And for me, having time to read is fun. Look, Greg's on his way, so I want to be available when he gets here, not in a show so he has to sit in the room by himself. Maybe when he gets in we can meet for drinks after the show and do some gambling?"

"Now that sounds like a plan." Justin took out his wallet and put a card on the bill. "That way everyone doesn't have to be so jealous of me being with the two prettiest women on the Strip."

"You're such a charmer." Amy smiled at her soon-to-be husband.

I stood. "I'm going to run back to the room and get my swimsuit on and grab my book. I'll text you as soon as Greg arrives, okay?"

"Sounds like a plan. We'll be out of the show around ten."

I left them talking about how excited they were to see the tigers, and I wondered if I should have gone with them. As I walked by the casino on the way to my room, I decided to go play some slots instead of reading. The level of alcohol in my system seemed to think it was a great idea too. I found one that looked like fun, with random bonuses, and sat down.

That was where Greg found me when he arrived at the hotel. "Winning?"

"I'm on the same twenty dollars. I get it up, lose a lot, then get it up again. Right now, I'm on an upswing, so I could cash out." I glanced at my watch. It was after ten. "You made great time. How's Emma?"

"Your dog is fine. She wanted to kick some butt when I let her outside. She lunged at the one guy who'd been trying to pick your lock. Good thing we got new locks and a security system installed a few years ago. He would have made short work of the old one." He took out a ten and slipped it into the machine next to me. I cashed out at just over a hundred, then put in another five and held on to the ticket.

We played as we talked about the break-in. When we cashed in our tickets and started walking to the room, I looked at him. "So why are you here?"

"I figured I wasn't making any progress on the case, so I might as well take some personal time and relax." He punched the elevator for our room. "I need to change into some clean jeans, but do you want to go grab a bite? I know you probably already ate, but I'm starving."

"I could eat. But I'm supposed to let Amy know when you're here so we could do something together tonight." I leaned against him in the elevator, feeling the strength I needed to go on. "Oh, and Mike Masters isn't a writer, he's a fed. And so was that real estate lady. They had to come back to Vegas for some meeting. I guess that's where they're stationed out of."

Greg spun me around and stared at me. "What are you talking about?"

I explained everything that had happened that night. When we reached the room, Greg pulled off his shoes. "I'll change into something a little warmer. If Amy and Justin want to go walking the Strip, I want some jeans and sneakers on."

"We're not leaving the room tonight. Text Amy and tell her I have to work. I'd appreciate it if you would order some room service. A burger would be fine, or anything you think I'd like. I heard the food here is pretty good." He went over and picked up his computer bag. "No alcohol. I want to get this done, then tomorrow we can turn off the rest of the world and celebrate with Amy and Justin."

"Was it something I said?" I went to the desk to find the room service menu.

"Actually, yes. If the feds have been involved in this investigation from the beginning, they might have some leads on why Frank was killed. And if it had something to do with their investigation, they can take this over. They're not good at sharing information, and I'm not having them play me like a fiddle. At least not anymore."

I scanned the menu. "You can get anything, including prime rib, through room service. I'm looking at the seafood pasta. I know I ate tonight with Amy and Justin, but I can't even remember what it tasted like. Except the first bite. Which was amazing."

He reached for the menu. "Get me a twelve-ounce T-bone, medium rare, baked potato, and veggies. Side salad with ranch. And something for dessert. Whatever you want half of. And two sodas."

"Sounds good." I ordered the food, then got into yoga pants and a long tee. I grabbed the second book out of my suitcase and curled up on the bed, waiting for room service.

When I tried to get settled, I saw Greg watching me. "What?"

"Sorry I grounded you. If I wasn't worried about this whole development thing, I'd send you out to play with your friends." He kept typing on his laptop as he talked.

"I kind of like spending the night in an upscale hotel with room service and guilt-free reading time. You aren't holding me against my will or anything."

"You're a good person, Jill Gardner. Maybe I should marry you one of these days."

I laughed, which apparently wasn't the reaction he'd expected. "That's the second time I've heard about the two of us getting married today."

"Your aunt pushing you?"

"Nope. Amy. She thought we could do the Elvis thing while we were down here." I snuggled deeper into the stack of pillows I'd set up and started reading. It was kind of the perfect end to the day. At least until the food arrived.

Chapter 21

The next morning, Greg filled me in. The feds hadn't known about Frank's death. Their field agents, Mike and Sara, had reported that Presley was starting up another scam, so that was why they were there, watching him. "Apparently, Mike has a habit of getting too involved in cases. His supervisor said he's been convinced that this Presley guy is attached to people here in Vegas who are connected."

"As in organized crime?" We were having our second room service–delivered meal. This time I had a large omelet stuffed with everything I loved. The orange juice had come with or without champagne. We had both chosen with, because Greg had declared this morning he was off duty until he was back in South Cove. We had a bread basket filled with amazing rolls and coffee cakes, as well as hash browns that were so crisp, they made me cry with joy. Yep, it was food heaven. "We are really going to have to check out the restaurants today before we join the party. I want to see what's out there."

"I can't believe you're planning more meals while we're eating breakfast." He held up a slice of ham. "Although this isn't half bad."

A knock came at the door, and when Greg went to answer, Amy and Justin came inside. Amy sat down on the bed next to me. "Ooh, coffee. Mind if I grab some? I think I had one too many margaritas last night."

Justin chuckled. "Actually, I think it was the shots. You can put down the tequila when you want to."

"It's my party and I'll drink if I want to." Amy grinned as she sipped the coffee. "We came to see if you wanted to grab breakfast, but I can see the answer to that question. We're going over to the Venetian to do the boats. You want to meet us there after we eat?"

"They have an art museum too. I want to see that. They're supposed to have some amazing pieces." I handed her a slice of banana bread.

"Sounds amazeballs." She ate the bread and almost chugged the coffee. "We had so much fun last night. You guys really should have come out too."

"I was the wet blanket, sorry," Greg admitted. "But today, there's no work. No one will even know I'm a cop."

"Sounds like a plan. After the chick stuff, maybe we can hit the roller-coaster over at New York-New York." Justin took a piece of Amy's bread. "This is amazing. We're getting room service tomorrow, sweetheart."

"Okay." She finished her coffee and popped up. "We'll see you at nine by the boats."

"We'll be there." I watched as they barreled out of the room and shut the door. The room was quiet. "They are two of a kind. They'll be perfect for each other."

"If you mean loud, outgoing, and always doing something, then yes, I agree with you." He leaned over and kissed me. "I think I'm going to be done people-ing after this vacation for a while."

"Me too." I refilled my coffee cup and scanned the list of restaurants from the travel magazine. "Apparently, the Venetian has one of the best breakfast buffets in town. We'll have to go over there tomorrow."

"Works for me." Greg said as he studied the sports page from the newspaper they'd delivered with breakfast.

I'd just finished eating and was eyeing the last piece of banana bread when my phone rang. It was Amy. I glanced at the time. We still had an hour before we were supposed to meet them. "Hey, I thought you said nine."

"You need to get over here. You won't believe who's here. He's got a babe on his arm." She paused. "I just sent you a text with a picture. Show it to Greg."

"Hold on." I waved him over to sit next to me. "Amy sent us a picture of someone we need to see."

When the text came up, Greg pointed to the woman. "That's California April Windsor—Frank's missing wife. We just got a photo from the driver's license bureau before I left the station. Who's that with her?"

"The man with his arm around her? That's Aaron Presley. The developer." I spoke back into the phone. "It's him, right?"

"Yep. It's him. He hasn't seen me because we're sitting in a different room, but I saw him when I went to find the ladies' room. I acted like I was taking a picture of the buffet."

"Tell Amy to stay there and we'll be right over. I'm going to get security involved because there is an active missing persons investigation on her." Greg pulled on his shoes and I relayed his message.

As we headed to the elevator, I grinned. "So much for no work this weekend, right?"

He leaned down and kissed me. "Sometimes it falls in your lap. I'll get security in on this, do a real quick interview, then figure out if I should be arresting her for killing Frank. If so, I'll have to do the whole extradition thing. If not, maybe I can just have her come to the station on Monday."

"Ever the optimist."

We power walked to the Venetian, which was farther than it looked. The good news was, the sidewalks weren't as crowded as they would be later in the day. When we got there, I went directly to the buffet and Greg went to the security desk. I had to pay to get in, which wasn't fair because I wasn't eating, but I grabbed a mimosa off the tray as I walked by and then sat at Amy's table.

"Where's Greg?" Amy glanced around nervously. "We don't have to go confront them on our own, do we?"

"No. Calm down. He's getting security involved. He'll talk to them and then we'll be done. Nice job, seeing them in this crowd." I took in the restaurant. People milled about the buffet lines. And the room smelled amazing. "I might just have to eat something, considering I had to buy my way in."

Amy pointed to the other room. We could just see their booth. Cali was standing up and leaving. "Oh, no."

I glanced at the entry area. No Greg, no security. Crap. I took a sip of my mimosa. "Text Greg and tell him she's on the move. I think she's probably just going to the restroom, but if she goes to her room or leaves the hotel, I'll text you."

"Be careful. She might be dangerous."

Cali was maybe five foot one and a size zero from what I could see. I wasn't worried about her taking me in a fight. I was worried about her disappearing again. I nodded to Amy. "Just text Greg. I'll keep my phone available and text as soon as I can."

I followed her out of the restaurant. So much for my second breakfast. That half of a mimosa had just cost me forty-five dollars. Maybe Greg could expense it and pay me back. The mayor would have a conniption. We went past the first restroom, but maybe she hadn't seen it. She was heading to the main lobby and out of the building. I hurried to get closer. If she got onto the street and hailed a cab, I would lose her. Maybe I could ask for directions and keep her on the street until Greg arrived. I saw her approach the main doors, but then she turned right. When I jogged up the few stairs, I realized where she was going. The art museum. I stood in line behind her to get a ticket and texted Greg our location. At least this way I'd get to do something I wanted at the same time as following our missing person. Multitasking was the best.

I was able to stay in the same studio as Cali for the next ten minutes. Then she sat down in front of a painting and took out a notepad. I glanced back the way we'd come. Still no Greg. What was he doing? I slipped onto the bench beside Cali and sighed. "It's so beautiful."

"Yes, it is." She smiled at me and returned to making notes. "It's a shame they're closing it down. I guess most people don't come to Vegas to see rare art."

"The hotel is beautiful, but sometimes, just sitting with a piece, you get to know so much more about the painting. Are you an artist?"

"Yes. I just had my first showing in San Francisco. It was at a very small gallery, but you have to start somewhere, right?" She dug into her pocket. "You can see my work on my website, here."

I glanced at the card. California Windsor—Artist. I guess this really was our girl. "I'm from California too. Nearby the city. It's a small town, you probably never heard of it. South Cove."

Cali dropped her pen. I reached down and handed it to her. When she didn't say anything, but sat staring at the painting, her hands shaking, I decided to jump in. "You know you're listed as a missing person, right?"

"I need to call the police and let them know where I am. My husband, Frank, he was killed in South Cove, but I'm thinking you already knew that." She turned to me. "You're the cop's girlfriend. The one with the historical wall on her property, right?"

"How did you know that?" I kept my eye on the doorway, just in case Greg finally showed up. I was getting a little nervous with the turn in the conversation.

She smiled and closed her notebook. "Frank used to talk about his projects. His finds, he called them. You were on the top of his list. He was so excited about finally proving the validity of your claim."

"Really? The Society closed our case."

I saw the response on her face. She'd known. "Look, it wasn't his fault, it was mine. I had some debt Frank hadn't known about. And when they came to me with a solution, I acted without telling him. He told me he would have paid the money. That he *could* have paid the money. I didn't think he had a dime to his name when I married him. But I guess he was better at hiding stuff than I was. Who knew he had fifty thousand tucked away?"

"Then *you* told him he had to cancel my wall's historical file. So the developer could buy the property."

"That was all I was supposed to do. Convince him to close it. When he said no, I pretended to be you, and I called to cancel it. Someone in the office besides Frank was in on it. They made sure the cancellation happened. Then Frank found out, and he was mad. He went to talk to you." She sighed. "When I heard about the accident, I freaked out. I came here and stayed in Aaron's condo. We met a few years ago and really hit it off. He's such a nice guy."

"Do you know what Aaron does for a living?" I could be wrong, but I had the feeling that Cali was one of those wrong-place-wrong-time people. Or she was trying to portray herself that way. Something about her story just wasn't ringing true.

"Something in real estate. Condos, I think. He's been busy here in Vegas and is just starting a new development in Reno." She frowned. "Why did you ask?" Before I could answer, she started, staring at a spot next to me.

Greg was at my side. "Miss Winston, I'm Greg King, lead detective of South Cove Police Department. Can I ask you if you drove here to Vegas?"

Cali shook her head. "I don't drive. Never have. I went to school in New York City and didn't need a car there. And I don't need one here. Or, I mean, at home in the city. Everything's right where I can walk."

"So how did you get here?" Greg's voice sounded kind, friendly. Just asking a few questions.

"Aaron came and got me. He flew me here in his private jet. The condo's so close to the Strip, it's like being at home." She shrugged. "I know I shouldn't be playing cards, but I love blackjack. I'm just on a strict budget this trip. Frank, well, he didn't approve of gambling."

"Were you and Frank still married?" I didn't know if Greg would ask, but I truly wanted to know.

She looked at me strangely. "Of course we were. I mean, we had our fights, but we were still working on our relationship. Now, well, now that he's dead, I guess it is what it is."

"Did you have a prenuptial agreement?" Greg was taking notes in the notebook he always carried. Even on vacation, I guessed.

"No. I told him if we got lucky and one of my paintings made me famous, he'd be a part of that, so I didn't insist on a prenup. I loved my husband." She pulled out a tissue and wiped her eyes. "I guess I'd better get back to reality and get everything situated. I can't hide in fantasyland forever."

I looked at Greg, but he shook his head. No need to tell Cali that Frank had left her a very rich widow. Frank's lawyer could do that.

He put away his notebook and took out one of his cards. "When you get back home, please call me. I have the name of Frank's lawyer and I think he'll need to talk to you about the final arrangements. I'm sorry for your loss."

"I am too." I stood up and stood by Greg. "If you want to talk, I'm at the bookstore in town most every morning. I'll buy you a cup of coffee."

We left her there, sitting and staring at the painting. It was of a simple house with several flowers in front and a bowl of fruit on an outside table. When we went back into the lobby of the Venetian, Amy and Justin were waiting for us.

"You didn't tell her she was rich," I said to Greg as we crossed the lobby to meet our friends. I wasn't quite sure Cali was telling me the entire truth. I mean, I wasn't in a position of authority or anything, and she'd spilled the story about making Frank kill my project for a developer. Didn't she know that was illegal?

"Leave that to the lawyer once she gets home. I don't want her going crazy in Vegas with the money. She seems like a good kid." Greg pulled me into a hug. "Sorry it took me so long to get there, but Aaron threw a little fit that got him arrested and in custody for the weekend. According to the Vegas cops who showed up, he shouldn't be able to get before a judge before Monday. So as soon as your aunt's dinner is over, I'm heading over to the jail to talk to him."

"And we get our weekend without any more interruptions." I squealed just a little.

"I'm not dumb. I know how to work a situation." He grinned at me. "So, we can check off the art gallery? Now it's time for a roller-coaster or two."

Justin jumped up. "Did someone say roller-coaster?"

* * * *

We played for the rest of the day. The party was starting at six, so when the clock struck five, we made our way back to our rooms. We parted ways in the elevator. We were on ten, but Amy and Justin were on a higher floor. "See you downstairs."

"We're going to have so much fun," Amy bubbled.

When we got into the room, I collapsed on the bed. "Tell me how much Amy would hate me if I just stayed in the room and watched television."

"She's your best friend. You can people for a few more hours for her." He opened his laptop. "If I have to play nice with the guys, you can go play with the girls." "We should disappear for a week. Just you and me. Maybe Emma." Greg didn't look up. "As soon as this case is closed, you've got it. Maybe a trip to Oregon to play on the dunes again?"

"I'm not sure I'd call our last Oregon trip relaxing. But I don't understand how someone comes to Vegas to relax." I closed my eyes. "There's too much to do and too much to see."

"And too many places to eat," Greg said. I could hear him typing on the keyboard. The man was a multitasking master.

"And definitely too many people," I added, curling up in a ball. I guess he let me sleep for a while, because the next thing I knew, he was shaking my arm and telling me I had thirty minutes to get ready. He knew I didn't need a lot of time. Which helped.

I dragged myself into the shower and tried to wake up. Cali's sad face kept coming to my mind. The poor girl. She'd been married less than a year, and now she was widowed. I wondered what the other wives got in the division of property. Frank seemed to be the type who liked to take care of others. But how in the world had she not known of his wealth? I guess she thought he worked full time for the Heritage Society and that was where he got his money. Greg and I were definitely having the money talk soon. Before this got any more serious. I didn't want him to think that the Miss Emily fund was part of the package. Right now, I used it for important things, like supplementing Nick's education costs. Or Sasha's childcare, so she could attend school. It was kind of like being an invisible Santa Claus. And I felt like the money was going to important projects. I didn't want to have to clear that with anyone, even Greg.

A discussion and a worry for another day. Right now, it was time to celebrate with my friend.

Chapter 22

Amy had chosen the learn-to-gamble package. We had our own minicasino, where we could play any of the casino games with a teacher/dealer by our side. And we all had a ton of fake money. At one part of the night, I was sitting at the blackjack table with my aunt. She was winning; me, not so much.

"You're too impulsive," she said after I'd lost the third hand in a row. "You need to lower your bet until your luck goes to your side."

"If I lose, I have to win bigger to make up for the loss," I countered. "It's math."

"Heaven help the shop if we ever have a downturn. You'll be broke before the economy can even start to turn around." She glanced down at the cards she'd pulled. Blackjack.

"That's the fourth, no, fifth blackjack you've hit since I sat down here." I looked at my cards. I had a two and a ten. Twelve. If I hit, I had a chance to bust. But the dealer had a nine showing, so I had to hit. I tapped the table. A pretty red queen added to my pile.

"Oh, too bad." The dealer turned over his other card and showed his nineteen. "But you had to hit. Either way, you would have lost."

"See. It's out of my hands." I put up my chip for another round. "Sometimes you're lucky and sometimes you aren't."

"Actually, I believe you make your own luck." My aunt put a hand on my arm. "You know I love you, right?"

Great, the gin and tonics were getting to her. Now she was going to tell me how much she hated my hair. Or Greg. No, it wouldn't be Greg. It would be one of my shortcomings. "Yes, and I love you too. This is an amazing way to kick off Amy's upcoming wedding, don't you think?"

"Actually, it's a young person's tradition. One last party. The thing people don't realize is, the parties that happen after your marriage are sweeter and more special." She smiled at me. "But I am happy for her and Justin. And you and Greg."

"Don't start. He hasn't asked and I haven't thought about it." I looked at my cards. I had twenty. So did my aunt. Maybe we'd both win this hand.

"He will. And I'm betting he will soon." When the dealer turned over an eight to go with his king, she smiled. "You should listen to me. I'm very lucky tonight."

"I always listen to you." Well, that wasn't always the truth, but it wasn't the time or place to talk business. Even though I was dying to find out who she'd hired. Maybe it was Jay's friend's daughter. I'd forgotten he'd said something about her needing a job. I couldn't stand it, and I'd had one too many beers just sitting here. I felt brave. "Tell me who you hired."

My aunt nodded to the dealer, who gave her a six to add to her fifteen and hit twenty-one. I'd passed on an eighteen. The dealer drew a seventeen. "The table wins," he announced.

My aunt pushed her chips into the dealer. "I'm heading to bed. Make sure you're downstairs at eleven thirty. And please wear something suitable. I'm not expecting formal wear, but maybe a nice dress? Tell Greg to dress up too."

"This restaurant is that fancy?" I sipped my beer and watched her. "Where are we going?"

"You'll find out."

I watched her cash in and realized she hadn't answered my question. I decided to leave it until Monday. Work could wait.

Amy sat down next to me. "This is so much fun. I love roulette. Who would have thought? And now I'm going to kick your butt in cards."

"Good night, girls," my aunt called as she left the room.

Amy looked at her and back to me. "Did I say something wrong?"

"Aunt Jackie has left the building." I nodded to the dealer. "She was just getting tired of winning. Let's see how lucky you are."

"I'm the bride. They have to let me win. It's in the contract." She squinted at the dealer, trying to read his name tag. "Isn't that right, Dave? Because I'm getting married on June 8, I get to win tonight."

"If you say so," Dave the dealer grinned. "Of course, I can't control the cards. What comes up, comes up."

"But the house is usually the winner, right?" I glanced at the automatic card shuffler. "There's no way to really win."

"Unless you have an amazing memory for five decks of cards, yes, the house has the better odds." He dealt our first hand. "But if you're just here for fun? The best way to win is to think you can. Be positive and upbeat, and the cards may go your way."

"That sounds like a self-help motto on how to live life." I glanced over at Amy. Her eyes were starting to glaze over. Thank God we weren't playing for real money or I'd call it and pour her into an elevator to go find her room. I was still going to have to do that later, but I was enjoying playing. And it made me wonder about Cali and her statement.

"Hey, just a question. Can people get underwater gambling? I mean, like totally spend their paycheck for the next year plus under?"

He nodded. "It's the bad side of the casino. They are supposed to cut people off when they get to a crazy level, but you can get under really quickly. And if you've been drinking the free alcohol, you may not realize just how many markers you've signed. I always try to send people to their room when they start looking like that."

I knew he was talking about Amy. "She's the bride this weekend. We'll let her play some more, and I won't let her out on the real casino floor. I'm in charge of her."

As I looked around the room, I realized that was the truth. No one else was still playing slots. Amy's cousins had disappeared, probably around the same time Aunt Jackie had gone to bed.

"Don't worry about the time." Dave noticed my scan of the room. "I'm paid until one no matter whether you or your friend leave. But if you don't think you'll need the others, I'll send them home."

"That will work." I smiled at my friend and pointed to her cards. "Blackjack. You did come lucky."

* * * *

By the time I got Amy to her room and into Justin's care, it was already one. He took her arm and led her away. "Thanks, Jill. You're the best."

I had lived up to my maid of honor responsibilities and now it was time to find my own room and get out of these shoes. While I waited for the elevator, I slipped them off and held the offending heels in my hand.

When I got on the elevator, a man already in the car chuckled. "Long night?"

"More like too high of heel. I'm used to flip-flops." I had considered putting on my sparkling, gem-encrusted flip-flops when I got dressed but changed my mind. Now I was going to have to wear these tomorrow too because my aunt wanted me looking "presentable."

"Flip-flops are cute." The man smiled at me and moved a little closer. "Of course, bare feet are the total turn-on."

I pushed the button for five. "Sorry, dude, my dance card is full."

He moved back away from me. "If you change your mind, my name is Dane and I'm here all weekend. I'll be at the blackjack tables. High roller section."

I wondered if that got him chicks. I got off on my floor and called back, "Have a nice night, Dane the high roller."

I heard his chuckle as the door closed.

Greg was still awake when I came into the room. He was watching sports on the television. I curled up next to him and watched the announcers go over a play that either was the best thing he'd ever seen or the worst, according to his panel mate. "Did you have fun? I can't believe you guys are already back from the party."

"Justin's friends all bailed. His brother couldn't get away because of some music gig. He tried to put on a good act, but he was bummed. Harrold turned in early. Toby picked up some cocktail waitress that was just getting off shift. She was going to show him 'the real Las Vegas.' Justin and I sat at the blackjack table until it went cold, then we came upstairs. How did you do?"

"About the same. Amy hired a learn-to-gamble room and we played with a lot of fake money all night. Aunt Jackie probably won enough on blackjack to finance a world cruise for her honeymoon. Too bad it wasn't real." I cuddled closer. "And I got hit on in the elevator."

Greg turned down the sound and turned toward me. "I'm sorry, what did you say?"

"Some high roller thought my bare feet were sexy, but I told him I was already spoken for." I pointed to the shoes I'd dropped by the door. "Those things are killer. I don't know how people actually walk in them."

"You're not supposed to walk far in them." He kissed me. "So was this guy cute?"

"Cute, rich, and had a great body. Why?"

Greg smiled down at me. "I'm just wondering why you came back to the room so soon. It's not like we're married or even engaged, right?"

"Believe me, bud, if I wanted to be somewhere else, I would be." I narrowed my eyes at him. "Why? Are you telling me you would have gone home with someone else? Just because we're not formally hitched?"

"Not on your life. Although I do think I'm going to have to do something so your hand doesn't look so naked. Even when your feet are bare." He leaned down and kissed me, and I forgot about Dane and the elevator and Vegas and even Amy and Justin.

* * * *

The next morning, the alarm blared, and I watched Greg roll over to turn it off. He shook my arm. "Time to get up."

"Why? We don't have to go anywhere. It's not noon, is it?" I tried to gauge the amount of sunlight, but we had pulled the shades last night.

"The buffet opens in thirty minutes. Do you want to go and actually eat something this time?" He started to lie back down. "Or we could just wait to eat at lunch."

I threw off the covers. "No way. I'll jump in the shower and I'll be ready in ten. Did you see the crab cakes Benedict on the sideboard?"

Thinking of food got me busy, and by the time Greg was out of the shower and dressed, I was flipping through my email, making sure Deek didn't have any issues. We have an alert at that bank that emails us about deposits—and withdrawals—and there had been two since I'd checked. Friday night and Saturday evening. The amounts looked normal, if a little high for a weekend day, but I wasn't going to complain. I closed the laptop with a snap and slipped on my flip-flops. "Are you ready?"

"Sure, let me grab my phone. You're really looking forward to this buffet, aren't you?"

"Darn right. I want to try one of everything." I slipped our room key in my tote. "And I'm sure that walking to the Venetian should counteract all the calories I'm getting ready to consume."

"Or not, but I won't tell if you don't." He frowned at a text. "Crap. There goes my witness."

"Did something happen? Do you need to handle it?" I wasn't going to be upset if he said yes. Well, I wasn't going to be visibly upset.

"Nothing I can do today. Someone came and bailed Aaron Presley out of jail. I guess my paperwork to question him in Frank's murder didn't get filed in time. He's in the wind now and I'll probably never close the Gleason case." He held the door open for me.

"Isn't that a little overdramatic? Maybe there's another way to pin him to the crime."

"If there is one, let me in on it. Right now, I'm out of ideas." He pushed the call button to the elevator. "I can't believe they didn't have better control on the guy."

We were crossing the street when I saw Cali. She was trying to flag down a cab and she had a man with her. "Is that Aaron?"

Greg took off running, dodging through the stopped traffic. "Call 911. Tell them that I'm in pursuit of a possible homicide suspect. And stay on that side of the street."

A woman standing next to me laughed. "I guess he told you, now, didn't he?"

I ignored her and dialed. When the dispatcher came on, I moved down the street to keep Greg and Cali in my sights. "I need a car dispatched to outside the Venetian. Greg King, police officer from South Cove, California, is in pursuit of a homicide suspect from South Cove."

"We have a substation in the Venetian. Our officers have been alerted and will be joining Detective King shortly. Can he keep the suspect under control until then?" the dispatcher responded. I was shocked. I'd thought I would have to explain who I was and why I was calling in a foot chase. "Ma'am? Is he near the suspect?"

"Greg can handle his own, but there are two of them." I didn't say one was a girl, but even girls could have a gun.

"Just stay on the line with me," the dispatcher tried to calm me.

I heard a scream. Not from Cali, but from Aaron. "Oh, thank God you're here, she's trying to kill me."

"Shut up," Cali screamed at him. "If you would have done this right, we would have been gone by now. But no, you had to stop at the casino for your lockbox."

"You idiot. How far did you think your inheritance was going to go once they figured out you were the one who masterminded Frank's death?" He pointed to his leg. "The witch shot me."

Now Cali was waving around a pistol. "For the last time, I didn't shoot you. This gun just went off. I hardly even touched the trigger."

Aaron's response was cut short by the sound of a shot. From Cali's gun. A window shattered in the building behind them. Then, before anyone could say anything, a team of black-suited men rushed behind Cali and took the gun from her hands. She was cuffed in record time. Then she and Aaron were taken inside the casino. I waited for the walk light, then sprinted after them. I caught Greg just as he was going into a door marked "Staff Only."

"Are you all right?" I hugged him. Then stepped back to make sure there weren't any bleeding holes in my boyfriend.

"I'm fine. Thanks for the assist. I was expecting a patrol car, but with that traffic, I don't think they could get through. Come on, let's see what our friends have to say." He put his arm around me and, as we walked down the plain hall, a voice came from my phone.

"Is everyone all right? Hello?" the dispatcher asked very loudly.

Greg took the phone from my hand. "This is Greg King, detective from South Cove, California. Thanks for sending your men in so quickly."

He listened and laughed. "Well, still, I appreciate the assist."

He hung up and handed the phone back to me.

"What did she say to make you laugh?"

He opened the door marked "Security" and motioned me to go ahead of him. "She said your call wasn't the weirdest one she'd had to deal with today. And she had just got on duty."

Greg checked in with the front desk and they started to lead him back to the cell area. He looked at me. "Go eat. I'll be along in a while."

The receptionist at the desk stood up. "I'll take you over to the buffet. And get you in as our treat. We appreciated the help you provided to apprehend the suspects. The alert just went out that these two have been suspected of stealing several pieces of art and multiple counts of identity theft."

I stepped toward her, then stopped and looked at Greg. "You'd better have this tied up by eleven. I'm not explaining to Aunt Jackie why you're late."

"I'll be there. I promise." He pointed to the door. "Go with the nice officer. You get grumpy when you don't eat."

"Whatever." Although I was starving, I didn't want him to think he was the boss of me or anything.

Chapter 23

My aunt brushed Emma hair off my dress with her hand. She really had gone all-out with one of her favorite Chanel suits. Harrold stood nearby, looking handsome in a black suit. Greg was wearing dress Dockers, but not a suit. I hoped they would forgive him. Or let him borrow a jacket if he needed one.

"Where did you say he was?"

Greg had arrived back at the room right at 11:15. I told him I'd come down and stall, but he needed to hurry.

I glanced at the elevators again. The door opened and Dane the high roller stepped out. He saw me watching and pointed to my feet. I saw him mouth the words, *Nice shoes.*

Then, from behind him, Greg came out of the elevator. His blue shirt and tie made him look friendly and approachable and totally hot. A smile creased my lips as I answered my aunt's question. "There he is."

He looked at Dane as he passed him by and then pointed back at him when he met me and drew me into a kiss. "Is that the guy I need to go beat up?"

"Why, because he found me totally irresistible?" I ran my hand down his chest. "You clean up good."

He smiled at me and twirled me so my dress flared out. "As do you."

"If you too are done canoodling, our ride has arrived." Harrold smiled at us, the skin around his eyes wrinkling.

"I guess I'm going to have to be the bigger man here, because I've got the girl." Greg put his arm around me, and we followed Harrold and Aunt Jackie outside and into a Mercedes Benz E-Class sedan.

"This is fancy." I settled my dress around me and glanced around. "I feel like I should have dressed up more."

"I told you to wear something nice," my aunt snapped. Then Harrold took her hand, and a look passed between them.

"You look lovely, Jill." He calmed the waters. Something he'd been doing a lot recently with my aunt. All I could think was thank God for Harrold.

"She does, doesn't she?" Greg put his arm around me. "I thought I was going to have to beat the other guys off with a stick this morning."

Trying to change the subject from foot fetish Dane, I looked out the window. "So, where are we going? I'm so excited about this lunch. Is it Wolfgang? Or Ramsay? Or one of the newer chefs?"

Harrold chuckled. "I think you'll be happy with the meal, but first, we have a stop to make."

I glanced at my watch. It was almost noon now. Good thing I'd eaten at the buffet after helping Greg apprehend the criminals. The whole morning had given me a huge appetite. "You're in charge of our little adventure; we're just along for the ride. I don't know if you heard, Greg arrested Frank's killer. Well, *killers*. I think she's going to claim he used her for access, but she's the mastermind, I know it."

"I think you're right." Greg explained the morning's events. "I was about ninety-nine percent sure this Aaron guy had either ordered the killing or drove the truck himself, but California gave me the rest of the whys. I can't believe they turned on each other so quickly. He was convinced she was going to kill him."

"She shot at him twice," I added. "And hit him in the leg. That would convince me."

"The problem with guns is, even an idiot can get lucky. We were lucky that second bullet went high. They found it in one of the angels decorating the ceiling in the lobby."

"Well, isn't that amazing. An angel saved people from harm. Isn't that the way it's supposed to work?" Harrold beamed. He always saw the positive side of things. Even when the angel was a statue and the bullet probably cost the casino thousands to get that section of lobby repaired.

The sedan pulled into a driveway and I looked out. All I could see was the next building, which appeared to be a strip mall where you could get tattoos while you waited. I wondered how a drop-off and pick-up tattoo worked? Someone needed to think about their marketing message.

I followed Harrold and Aunt Jackie out into the heat of midday and gasped. The official Elvis Wedding Chapel was on the other side of the strip mall.

And that's where we were headed.

My aunt took my arm. "Don't dawdle in the parking lot. You'll melt. Besides, our appointment is in a few minutes."

Entering the lobby, Mary and Bill Sullivan stood up and greeted us. "We drove up first thing this morning and will stay the night at the same hotel," Mary explained. "From the look on your face, Jackie hasn't told you their surprise yet."

I turned to my aunt. "You're getting married? Here? No huge wedding. No wedding planner book. No choosing linens?"

Harrold laughed, and my aunt shot him a look. "Harrold and I decided we were ready to get on with our lives. Besides, I can't be living with a man without being married to him. It would be scandalous."

Greg reached out and slapped Harrold on the back. "Congratulations. If you'd told me last night, I would have bought you a shot."

"I had enough liquor last night. Besides, that was Justin's party. He needs the courage to get through all of Amy's planning. He's going to be one relieved man when they finally get to the honeymoon." Harrold greeted Bill and Mary.

Aunt Jackie pulled me aside. "Did you open that box I left for you at the shop?"

I'd actually forgotten about it. She must have seen the answer on my face. She took my hand.

"It's just a few things I thought you might like. I didn't want to carry the physical memories of my first marriage into my second. I loved your Uncle Ted. And I love your new Uncle Harrold. Love isn't stingy that way. And there are a few things you might want for when you make it official with that guy." She pointed to Greg. "I've never seen you so happy. Don't waste this time."

I hugged her and promised I'd retrieve the box as soon as we got back to town. A man dressed as Elvis came out of the chapel. "I take it we're all here? Who's the lucky bride and groom?"

Harrold took my aunt's arm in his and stepped toward Elvis. "We are."

"Then let's get this party rocking!" He froze in a position that appeared to be Elvis playing a guitar, then popped up. "Thank you, thank you very much for choosing our chapel."

Greg took my arm, and we followed Mary and Bill into the flower-covered chapel. Toby and Herman showed up just before the ceremony started.

The chapel and the ceremony were beautiful, and we stood with the others as Aunt Jackie and Harrold took their vows. To love, to honor, and I noticed the Elvis preacher dude took out the word "obey." Which was probably for the best. My aunt didn't obey anyone. She did anything she wanted, and always out of love.

During lunch, Bill pulled me aside. "I didn't want to bring this up before the festivities, but I want you to know the Council is sending out a revision letter about the fee increases and apologizing if the last letter made it seem like we blamed you or your shop."

A wave of relief ran through me. I couldn't believe how much this had been affecting me. "Alice Carroll is a menace. She tried to close me down."

"I believe she was acting under the impression that she'd get the commissions from the land sales if the water park went through. Your house was a kingpin piece for the whole development. Your property provided the access to the road. So, if you didn't sell, the project wouldn't go through." He pointed at Greg. "And I have it on good authority that she might just be charged in some form for Frank's death. Accessory after the fact, I think it's called."

"She needs to go to jail. I wouldn't have sold the house even if my business had gone down." I glanced around at my friends and family. Amy and Justin had joined us for the celebration lunch, which was being held in a banquet room at the Venetian. Not the famous chef I'd been expecting, but the food was amazing. "That's my home. You don't walk away from home."

Bill must have heard my subtext, because he hugged me. "And that's why people like Alice and this developer guy will never win. They don't get that one statement."

Chapter 24

The staff meeting was scheduled for Tuesday at seven in the morning. I'd already had most of my commuters, and I'd serve them as the rest came in. My aunt was directing Deek on how to set up the tables. And Toby was getting the treats set up. Today, we also had orange juice and a bottle of champagne to celebrate my aunt's impromptu wedding. We had just all sat down and were chatting about the weekend when a woman came in the front door.

"I'll be right back." I stood and started to go to the counter.

My aunt touched my arm. "Sit down, Jill. That's not a customer."

The woman walked over and took the empty seat. It was the woman who'd been hanging out at the shop the last few weeks. "Sorry I'm late. I brought a load of stuff to start moving into the apartment this afternoon, if that's okay? My dad took the day off, so he's back at the house packing up my stuff. I think he's just happy to get rid of me and Homer."

"Not a problem. Everyone, this is our newest Coffee, Books, and More staff member. Evie Marshall. She's also going to be renting the apartment upstairs." She turned to me. "Evie, this is my niece, Jill."

"I've heard so much about you." Evie reached over and shook my hand. "So excited to be part of the team."

"I haven't heard anything about you. Are you Jay's neighbor's daughter?"

Toby kicked my chair. "No, she's not Jay's neighbor's daughter. I can't believe you don't see the resemblance. Nice to see you again, Evie."

I considered the woman as she said good morning to Deek and Toby. She was strikingly beautiful. Her dark skin highlighted her green eyes. And her braids were loose today. She used beads in her hair like Deek used color on his blond dreadlocks. She did look like someone, but who?

Then it came to me. Olivia. She looked like a grown-up version of Olivia. "You're related to Sasha?"

The woman laughed. "She's my cousin. She always ranted on and on about what a great place this was to live and work, so when my divorce was final, South Cove was the first place I thought of to regroup."

"And Homer is your son? How old is he?" I wondered what it would be like having a kid running around upstairs. I hoped he liked to read.

"Fourteen, but he acts like he's two." She laughed and poured herself some coffee. "I'm looking forward to being so close to the beach. He loves the waves."

"She has a Pomeranian." My aunt looked at me. "I told her it was okay to bring him along."

"Oh, Homer is a dog." Okay, so I *am* more of a Captain Obvious than my aunt.

"Now that the introductions are done, I wanted to talk about Evie's training. She'll be taking over the midday shift while Harrold and I are on our cruise next month. Deek, you'll be closing. Will that interfere with your classes?"

"Only one. I can't close on Wednesdays." He looked at me, but Toby spoke up.

"I can close for you those days. Just put me on the schedule."

And that's how the meeting went. Everyone was thoughtful and supportive. Even though I knew it wouldn't last, I kind of liked this gentler version of our staff meetings. Aunt Jackie didn't do her typical minitraining of things they already knew. But she did read the reversion letter of the increased dues out loud to the group. And Bill had put in an apology from the Council to our store and our employees.

"I heard that Alice Carroll resigned her position," Aunt Jackie said after folding the letter back into the envelope.

"Yeah, but she said it was because she was moving her real estate business. I think having a DUI in the town where you need to sell houses puts a question mark on your character," Deek added his bit of gossip.

"And I was the one who caught her," Toby crowed. "You're all welcome. 'Ding Dong! The Witch Is Dead.'"

"I'm just glad the shop's not being attacked. I was expecting a swarm of locusts next." I leaned back in my chair and sent up a silent thank you to Bill for his assistance.

After they'd left, I pulled out the box that had been under the counter. Aunt Jackie's first wedding memory book, a dried flower, a picture of me from my first wedding. And, as I opened the jewelry box, a set of worn wedding rings in gold. Uncle Ted's was a plain wide band. My aunt's rings were a matched set, with a small diamond and three even smaller stones on the wedding ring.

"We were going to replace the stone for our twentieth anniversary," my aunt said from behind me. She leaned on my shoulder and reached around to touch the rings. "But he didn't make it. I know some people let the rings go with them, but your Uncle Ted wasn't in that casket."

I looked at her sharply. "He wasn't?"

She shook her head. "Once his spirit was gone, I barely recognized the body at the funeral. Don't look at me that way. I know it was your uncle's body. But his spirit, it had moved on."

"Are you sure you don't want these?" I held up the ring box.

She stepped away and looked down at the ring with the much larger stone she'd taken on Sunday. "No. That part of my life is over. Now, it's a new chapter. One with Harrold. By the way, I need to tell you something."

Now what? I kept my face neutral and put away the rings and the box in the office. I'd take them home with me today and put them away in my office safe. "Oh?"

"Harrold wanted you to know that you and I are not in line to inherit the shop. Well, not unless his son and children pass before you. And I informed him that my share of Coffee, Books, and More wouldn't go to him, it would revert back to you." She touched the ring. "He's set up a fund for me in case something happens. I'll be well taken care of. As long as some charlatan doesn't get his hands on my money again."

"I don't think you'd let that happen again. You learned your lesson." I filled a cup of coffee and handed it to my aunt.

"I definitely hope so. You know it wasn't long ago that I thought Ted might be alive. If you hadn't stepped in…"

"You would have figured it out. You're a smart woman. I'm just here to catch you when you need help." I poured my own coffee. "Evie seems nice."

"Sasha called a few weeks ago and asked if we would have room for her. I couldn't turn the girl down. She's been through a lot."

"You're a softy." I smiled at my aunt. "A big, fat softy."

She shuddered. "Don't let that get around. I need to go and walk through the apartment one last time. I think Evie should be moved in by the end of the day."

I watched my aunt as she took her coffee with her upstairs. It would be different, having a new person living in the apartment. But change happens in life. Good changes and bad changes. Nothing ever stays the same.

As a customer walked into the store, I smiled and called out a welcome. Yes, changes happen. And I wouldn't want it any other way.

A Note From Lynn

Dear Reader,

I know Jill and the rest of my characters talk about food. A lot. However, for me, food is an important part of living. My husband? Not so much. Don't get me wrong, he likes a good meal. But as long as he's not hungry, he's satisfied. Me, on the other hand, I like food. And eating something just to eat makes me sad. I was delighted when I tried this low-carb, high-protein, easy breakfast treat.

There are several different versions, and I'm always substituting different veggies based on what's in my refrigerator at the moment. Here's the basic recipe. Go crazy and try some new ingredients if you want. And be sure to let me know at my Facebook author page what worked and what didn't.

Lynn

Recipe

Easy, Low-Carb Egg Muffins
Beat together:
6 large eggs
3 tbsp. milk
Salt
Pepper
½ tsp. garlic powder
Spray a metal cupcake tin (12 slots) with cooking spray, then layer in the cups
8 slices Canadian bacon, chopped
½ bunch green onions, chopped
5–6 large white mushrooms, sliced
1 cup chopped green peppers (or a mix of red and green)
½ cup shredded cheddar cheese

Pour the egg mixture over the cups, making sure to spread it out evenly.
Bake in a 350 degree oven for 30-35 minutes.
Cool. Package in an air-tight container and refrigerate.
Then, tomorrow morning, pop two out onto a plate and microwave 30 seconds to 1 minute.
Enjoy with a cup of fresh fruit for a quick breakfast.

Tourist Trap Mysteries

There's plenty more to come in South Cove
in the next Tourist Trap Mystery
Coming Soon!
And don't miss more mysteries from
Lynn Cahoon
in the Farm-to-Fork series
and the Cat Latimer series
Available now!

Printed in the United States
by Baker & Taylor Publisher Services